MISADVENTURES OF A COLLEGE GIRL

BY
LAUREN ROWE

MISADVENTURES

OF A

COLLEGE GIRL

BY
LAUREN ROWE

WATERHOUSE PRESS

To Sophie. Both of them. I love you.

PROLOGUE

My stomach is doing somersaults. I stare at my computer screen, reading the words of my admissions essay to NYU one final time.

Dear Sir or Madam,

The first time I read Romeo and Juliet, it made me ponder the role of fate versus free will in my own life. Is my fate written in the stars as it was for Romeo and Juliet, or do I have the power to forge my own path, paved with my deepest desires? Juliet declares, "O Fortune, Fortune! All men call thee fickle. If thou art fickle, what dost thou with him. That is renowned for faith?" I'm paraphrasing here, but Juliet then goes on to beg fickle Fortune to keep its grubby paws off Romeo because, well, he's a great guy and she loves him. Obviously, fickle Fortune didn't wind up heeding Juliet's plea. But, hey, points for trying.

I'm not sure why Romeo and Juliet has always resonated with me so much. Maybe it's because my own parents were star-crossed lovers. My mother died in a car accident when I was two, and I truly believe my father would have followed his young wife into the grave were it not for the toddler she left behind for him to raise. A little girl with blue eyes and a dark mop of curly hair who was the singing-and-dancing spitting image of his ill-fated Juliet. Or perhaps I was so fascinated by Romeo and Juliet because, by all accounts, my mother loved me more than life itself. And yet, when it came down to it, her love wasn't enough to persuade fickle Fate to keep its grubby paws off her.

I take a deep breath at those last words. But I press on.

I'm honestly not sure what I've concluded about the role of fate versus free will in my life. But I'm convinced that, whether everything is predetermined or not, I belong at NYU. I've believed NYU to be my future alma mater since my grandparents took me to visit New York City at age ten and told me that attending your fine university had once been their ill-fated daughter's dream. But even if my attendance at my dream school isn't written in the stars, then I implore you to take me anyway, if only to settle the fate-versus-free-will debate, once and for all. What better way to show fickle Fate who's boss, right?

I know I'm a small-town girl from Nebraska, and you have the entire world of talented applicants to choose from. Indeed, the smallness of my life sometimes feels like an immutable gravity, weighing down my very soul. But I'm writing this application because I know in my molecules I'm meant to defy gravity. Not just for myself, but for my mother, too.

In another part of this application, I've submitted my grades and test scores for your review, and I think you'll conclude based on those numbers, I've got the brains and work ethic to excel at NYU. With this essay, I'm hoping to convince you of something far more important: I've got the heart and soul, too.

Thank you for your consideration,

Zooey Cartwright

I stare at my computer screen for a long moment, holding my breath, and finally press Submit. Instantly, the enormity of what I've just done slams into me. I throw my hands over my face. "O, I am Fortune's fool!" I blurt, quoting Romeo.

"Huh?" my dad says from the couch. He's watching a football game on TV. Eating Doritos. Drinking a beer. "What'd you say, Zo?"

I clear my throat. "Nothing. I'm just being a dork, Dad. Carry on."

Dad returns to his game and Doritos, completely unfazed. I don't blame him. I act like a dork quite frequently.

When I'm sure my dad's attention is focused on the TV again, I steeple my hands under my chin, close my eyes, and whisper in the tiniest voice possible so my sweet father, a Nebraska man through and through who's never understood his daughter's obsession with all things New York City, won't overhear me. "Please, God," I whisper. "Let me get into my dream school. And then, please, if you're feeling particularly magnanimous, help me figure out a way to pay for it, too."

CHAPTER ONE

"I don't know how you've held out this long, Zooey," my new roommate in the dorms, Clarissa, says. "If I were still a virgin at this point, I think my clit would explode like a rocket at lift-off every time I so much as *looked* at a hot guy."

"That's quite a visual."

We both giggle.

It's a warm September evening, two days before the start of classes at UCLA, and I'm sitting in my new dorm room at Hendrick Hall with my randomly assigned roommate, telling her things I've never told anyone, not even my best friends back home. Why am I divulging my most intimate secrets and fantasies to a girl I've known for two days? I have no idea. All I can figure is Clarissa Michaelson must be some kind of witch, because I simply can't resist opening up to her.

"Is being an eighteen-year-old virgin *that* weird out here in California?" I ask. "Back home it's not that weird."

"It's probably about fifty-fifty, I'd guess. I'm just saying if it were *me*, I'd be losing my mind. But that's just 'cause I've always been insanely boy-crazy."

"Oh, so have I," I say. "I just haven't been able to act on my boy-craziness because my dad's always been super strict with me. But now that I'm finally away from home, I'm going to let my boy-crazy run amok, come hell or high water."

"What Daddy doesn't know won't hurt him."

"Amen. So how did you lose your virginity?"

"Exactly the way a 'nice girl' is supposed to do it—with my high school boyfriend who loved and respected me." She snickers. "And, oh my God, it was such a letdown! He was insanely hot, too, so I figured he'd rock my world. But nope. He was a total dud."

My heart is racing. I've never had such a frank and open conversation about sex in my life. "What made him such a dud?"

Clarissa makes a comical face. "Well, first off, the boy wouldn't have known a clitoris if it bit him on the ass."

"Yet another interesting visual."

We both giggle again.

"And second off..." She holds up her pinky suggestively, making me laugh for the hundredth time. "I mean, from my own experience and what my friends have told me, the first time pretty much sucks for most girls. It's just too big a freak-out to have a dick inside you for the first time. So I guess I can't blame my boyfriend too much for that first time not being spectacular. But it never got much better, even after two months. And you want to know the most aggravating part? My boyfriend kept going on and on about how 'amaaaaazing' sex was with me." She rolls her eyes. "So glad *he* enjoyed it. Would have been nice if he'd noticed I was lying there counting the ceiling tiles. So, anyway, I eventually lost interest in him and we broke up." Her face lights up. "And that's when I finally discovered what it feels like to have fantastic sex." She smiles devilishly. "I went to this party and wound up hooking up with this basketball player douchebag from my high school. A *total* womanizer. But every girl he'd slept with—and there were lots—said, 'Yeah, he's a douchebag, but I'd do him again in a heartbeat.' So I figured I'd give him a whirl and see if my lack of Os with my boyfriend was a him thing or a me thing."

I lean forward on my small bed, holding my breath with anticipation. "And?"

"And, holy shit, girl! It was a him thing! I had *three* orgasms with the douchebag our first time out! I hadn't had *one* in two months with my boyfriend! Not *one*." She sighs happily. "Man, that douchebag was good."

I feel flushed. "Is sex *that* different depending on the guy?"

"Oh, honey. It's the difference between an opera singer belting out Mozart and a tone-deaf dude singing 'Happy Birthday' to his sister."

We both shriek with laughter.

"That's the day I discovered all dicks and tongues and fingers are *not* created equal, my friend. Not. At. All."

I fan myself. "Is it suddenly getting hot in here?"

Clarissa giggles. "So that's why I say, if you're truly thinking about losing your V card the way you've been telling me, then you should find yourself a de-virginizer who knows exactly what he's doing. Nice boys with little to no experience need not apply, no matter how hot they might be."

"But how on earth would I know in advance if a guy's good at sex? It seems like a total crap shoot, especially at a school this big. There are over thirty thousand students at UCLA. I wouldn't even know where to start looking for the rumor mill regarding a particular guy."

"Yeah, good point. It's probably a lot easier to get intel on guys in high school." She twists her mouth, seemingly deep in thought. "But I'd think you could drastically increase your odds of finding a guy who knows what he's doing by looking for certain telltale signs."

"Like what?"

"Well, for instance, if a guy's a great kisser, he'll likely be good at sex, too. Not guaranteed, but it's a good start. Also, you should probably go against your usual instinct when scouting the guy. I'm assuming you're the kind of girl who typically crushes on nice boys who are classic boyfriend material?"

I nod. She's got me pegged.

"Okay, then look for guys you'd normally sprint away from at full speed—the ones who make it blatantly obvious they're womanizers."

"How do guys make it obvious they're womanizers? Sorry, I'm lame."

"They just do. When you see a guy like that, you'll know it. They've got this *swagger*."

I shudder with excitement. "Man, I *really* want to do this, Clarissa."

"Then do it. No big whoop."

"It's not that simple."

"Sure, it is."

I feel myself blushing. "I'm nervous I'll be bad at it and embarrass myself." I bite my lip, take a deep breath, and just spit it out. "I've never had an orgasm."

Clarissa tilts her head to the side. "You mean never, *ever*? Or just with a guy while fooling around?"

My cheeks flash with color. "Never. I've tried to make it happen on my own, but..." I sigh. "I think I'm defective. Either that or I'm doing it wrong."

Clarissa asks me a bunch of embarrassing questions, but based on the lack of judgment I'm seeing on her face, I feel emboldened to answer all of them with complete honesty.

"Nothing to be embarrassed about," Clarissa declares when I'm done telling her the details of my paltry solo efforts and the few make-out sessions I've had. "Everyone starts in your exact shoes at some point."

I sigh with relief. "God, I love talking to you about this," I admit. "I've never talked to anyone about this stuff before."

"Not even your mom? I mean, not in detail, but just, you know...the basics?"

I don't normally talk about my late mother right off the bat with new people. But the look of pure kindness on Clarissa's face makes me want to bare my soul to her without holding back. "My mom died in a car accident when I was two," I say softly.

Clarissa looks stricken. "I'm so sorry, Zooey."

"Thank you. It's sucked growing up without a mom, but my dad's done a great job. He's *way* too protective of me for my taste, but he's always been really sweet."

"I'm surprised your dad let you go to school so far from home if he's so protective."

"He wanted me to go to the University of Nebraska. He played football there. Actually, my lifelong dream was to go to NYU, but I didn't get in. Which is crazy, by the way. It's supposed to be way harder to get in here. But go figure."

"It's such a crapshoot. If it weren't for water polo, I doubt I would have gotten in here."

"Who knows? So, anyway, when I got accepted here with a partial scholarship, my dad couldn't say no to an opportunity like that, even though I'm sure he was totally freaking out."

Clarissa comes to sit on my bed and hugs me. "I'm so glad we got assigned as roommates, Zooey. I was nervous I'd get someone lame, and it turns out I got my future best friend." She pulls away from our embrace. "Hey, you want to go to our first college party tonight? You never know—you might find yourself a talented douchebag to kiss."

"Let's do it," I say. "What party?"

"This morning at the bookstore, this sweet guy told me about a party being thrown by a bunch of football players. It's perfect. Football players are notorious for being womanizers. Maybe one of them will catch your eye and turn out to be a fantastic kisser and...who knows where that might lead?"

"You don't think a bunch of football players would be annoyed if two random freshmen crashed their party?"

"Ha! Zooey, freshmen girls can't crash a party, even if we wanted to—we're always implicitly invited." She snorts. "But, regardless, the guy from the bookstore expressly invited me, and he's the quarterback's tutor."

"Sounds great," I say. "But fair warning, flirting with a bunch of football players is going to be way outside my comfort zone. I'm not naturally outgoing like you."

"But you're a theater major."

"It makes no sense, I know. Put me in a costume and give me a script and I'm fearless—ask me to be myself with new people, and I take some time to warm up."

"Well, then, we'll just have to put you in a costume and give you a script. Easy peasy." She looks me up and down. "Speaking of costumes, honey, this whole 'small-town virgin' thing you've got going on definitely doesn't scream 'I'm a hot vixen looking for a meaningless hook-up!' If you want to attract a guy like that basketball player douchebag of mine from high school, you'll probably want to tamp down the 'I'm your future wife!' vibe."

We both laugh.

"You're beautiful, Zooey," Clarissa says, her tone sincere. "A natural beauty. But for your stated mission, I'd suggest you lead with your sexuality a bit more."

"I wouldn't even know how to begin to do that."

"I'd be happy to help you, if you'd like. A head-to-toe makeover and you'll get the attention of every football player at the party tonight, no doubt."

I bite my lip, considering.

"No pressure, of course," Clarissa adds quickly. "I'm only offering because you said it's what you want to do. But it's *your* V card. Your body. I don't have a horse in this race. All I'm saying is if this is what you want, then I'll help you."

"Oh, I want to do it," I say firmly, and it's the truth. "One hundred percent. I've felt like a horny prisoner in a cage for the past year, and I'm ready to break out, baby."

Clarissa guffaws.

"Do whatever you want to me, Mr. Miyagi," I declare,

nodding emphatically. "I'm your Karate Kid."

"Okey dokey." Clarissa looks at her watch. "*Oh*. We'd better get moving. We've only got about four hours before the party, and there's tons I've got to do to you."

"You've got four *hours'* worth of stuff to do to me? What on earth could possibly take so long?"

"Wax on, wax off." She snickers. "In your case, literally."

I grimace. "You sure that's necessary? I've heard waxing is painful for first-timers."

"Oh, it is." She smiles sweetly. "It's brutal. So I suggest you take a couple ibuprofen before we get started." She indicates my thick, curly hair. "If your carpet matches your drapes at all, this isn't going to be pleasant for you."

CHAPTER TWO

Hip-hop is blaring so loudly in this living room, my molars, eyeballs, and ovaries all feel like they're thumping in time with the bass-heavy beat. A thick blanket of smoke hangs in the air, refracting colored beams of light shooting across a makeshift dance floor. And people, people, people—almost all of them holding red Solo cups or beer bottles—are packed into every nook and cranny of the cramped space. In other words, I've found heaven on earth.

Clarissa leans in to my ear and shouts to be heard over the loud music. "Lots of potential cherry-poppers here, huh? Wowzers!"

I nod effusively. That's an understatement. There are more potential cherry-poppers in this one cramped room than attended my entire high school back home. "Pop, pop, pop!" I shout into Clarissa's ear.

Clarissa taps her ear, telling me she didn't understand the stupid thing I just said, and I swat at the air to tell her never mind.

"Anyone catch your eye?" Clarissa shouts into my ear.

Why, yes. Without hesitation, I indicate a tall, blond, muscular guy I've been drooling over for the past five minutes, ever since we arrived, though I'm certain he hasn't noticed I

18

exist. "The golden god!" I shout. "Blue shirt!"

Clarissa looks to where I'm pointing across the room, and her eyes bug out of her head. She nods effusively and gives me a thumbs-up with both hands. "He looks like a superhero!"

"Totally!" I peek at him again and swoon. "It's wishful thinking, I know, but a girl can dream!"

Clarissa taps her ear, yet again, and I gesture, telling her to forget it.

Clarissa leans toward my ear. "Let's talk in the kitchen!"

And off we go, working our way through the packed crowd. As we walk, I can't help noticing more than one dude brazenly checking me out. Almost immediately, I lock eyes with a hottie with sparkling brown eyes...but then immediately look down, my cheeks bursting with heat. When I look up again, Brown Eyes is gone, supplanted by a different hottie who happens to be, at this moment, staring at my boobs. When the second hottie's eyes migrate to mine, he flashes me a panty-melting smile...and I immediately look down again.

When I look up a third time, a Hawaiian-looking guy in a backward baseball cap is giving me the once-over. *Wow.* Clarissa didn't over-promise when she said she could make me into a hottie-magnet tonight. Frankly, I don't blame all these boys for checking me out. If I were a horny college guy, I'd check me out in this body-baring dress, too. But it's not my revealing dress alone that's transformed me into a hottie-magnet tonight. It's my hair and makeup, too. I had no idea my face could be painted to look this *mysteriously bitchy.* Or that my curly hair could be straightened into the kind of smooth-as-silk mane I've always envied on models in shampoo commercials. If anyone back home saw me looking like this tonight, they wouldn't even recognize me. Which suits me just fine, of course, considering my rather scandalous mission for the evening.

Clarissa and I enter the kitchen and begin chatting excitedly about all the potential cherry-poppers in the other room, especially the golden god. But before we've finished our conversation, an adorable, nerdy guy approaches and enthusiastically greets Clarissa. After introductions and small talk, I find out this sweet guy is the one who invited Clarissa to the party, and his name is Dimitri. A little more conversation and we learn he's a third-year biochemistry major with a minor in creative writing.

"Clarissa told me you tutor a player on the team?" I say.

"Several." Dimitri points out a couple of large guys standing around a keg on the far side of the kitchen. "And I also tutor the quarterback, Jake Grayson." He looks around. "Hmm. I don't see Jake in the kitchen. He must be in the other room." Dimitri describes Jake, and it's immediately clear he's talking about the golden god.

"So is Jake single?" Clarissa asks, but when Dimitri's darling face visibly falls, she quickly adds, "For Zooey. She saw him in the other room and went all weak in the knees."

Dimitri smiles knowingly. "Yeah, that's pretty much the universal female reaction to seeing Jake for the first time." He looks at me. "He's single, as far as I know. He was telling me a couple days ago that he'd just broken things off with his high school sweetheart from back home. I'd be happy to introduce you to him, if you'd like. He's a junior. Great guy. Not a whiff of the usual athlete-womanizer-God-complex cliché with him. He's definitely a humble, one-woman sort of guy."

At that last comment, Clarissa and I exchange deflated looks that say, *Dang it.*

"I can't say the same about some of the other guys on the team," Dimitri continues, rolling his eyes. "I mean, lots of players are funny and entertaining, super-fun guys to hang out with and all. But when it comes to women, holy crap, they're just shamelessly on the prowl twenty-four seven. The thing I don't get is why otherwise sane girls throw themselves at guys like that when..."

I've stopped listening to Dimitri. And I've stopped breathing, too. A tall, dark-haired slab of male perfection just strutted into the kitchen and commanded my full attention. *Oh, sweet Jesus.* Who the hell is that? He's gorgeous, though in a totally different way than the golden god in the other room. If Mr. Quarterback is Thor, then this hunk of brazen sexuality is Loki. If the golden god is sunshine, this dude is moonlight. If Jake in the other room is my future husband, then this guy blazing his way through the kitchen is the stripper I'd screw as my last hurrah during my bachelorette party in Vegas. *Well, winner, winner, chicken dinner.*

My future one-night stand has dark hair, muscles, and tattoos. A strong jawline with a hint of stubble. Not to mention a truly ridiculous body clad in jeans and a tight black T-shirt, which shows off his broad shoulders and bulging arms. Now, to be fair, the golden god in the other room has a ridiculous body, too. But something about the cocky way this guy carries his bountiful assets tells me and everyone within fifty yards of him he knows exactly how to use what the good lord gave him in ways the golden god doesn't.

Oh, fuckity. He's walking in my direction and making my heart pound harder and harder with each step he takes. Finally, when he's mere feet away from me, I'm able to make out the white lettering emblazoned across his black T-shirt. God's Gift to Womankind. That's what Loki's T-shirt says! *Ha!* I roll my eyes to myself. And to think I'd been nervous I wouldn't be able to spot a womanizer at this party.

Mr. God's Gift to Womankind stops walking to chat with a group of people, and they high-five him and pat him on the back like he's the second coming of Christ.

I grab Clarissa's arm and lean in to her ear. "Dark hair. Tattoos. Black shirt. Everyone's fawning all over him." I indicate with my elbow. "Read his T-shirt. Total douchebag."

Clarissa follows my gaze toward the guy...at the exact moment he turns his head away from his group...*and looks straight at me.* Shocked, I look down at my hands, my heart clanging. Holy hell, that was quite a smolder that boy just directed at me. *Damn.*

"Zooey," Clarissa whispers into my ear, poking my arm. "He's looking right at you. Look at him!"

But I can't muster the courage. The smolder Loki aimed at me was so sexual, it flash-melted the cotton crotch of my panties.

Clarissa nudges me again. "He's ogling you! Ogle him back!"

"I suck at flirting," I murmur. "I warned you."

"Oh, for God's sake." She grabs my forearm and leans in

to me. "Now listen to me, Karate Kid. Stare that hottie down right freaking now for a slow count of five. Look into his eyes and think this exact thought—I want to suck your dick. Now do it!"

I take a deep breath, channel my inner vixen, and look up, resolved to follow my master's rather shocking instructions... but, dammit, *no*! God's Gift to Womankind isn't looking at me anymore. He's on the move, working his way through the crowded kitchen, fist-bumping and high-fiving admirers as he goes. "Crap," I whisper to Clarissa. "I blew it."

"No, no. That was just round one," Clarissa says. "That boy's not even close to done with you yet."

Dimitri wraps up a conversation he's been having with that Hawaiian-looking dude from the other room and then returns his attention to us. "What'd I miss?"

"Nothing much," Clarissa says. "We were just talking about our classes."

"What classes are you ladies taking this quarter?"

Clarissa takes one for the team and launches into telling Dimitri about her class schedule so I can continue eyeball-stalking God's Gift to Womankind across the kitchen. I peek in his direction and...Gah! He's staring right at me again! Standing at the keg in the corner with a group of athletic-looking guys *and staring right at me*!

My inner voice is screaming at me to look away. But I force myself to maintain eye contact and follow Mr. Miyagi's instructions to a tee. Slowly, I count to five, my eyes locked with his. *I want to suck your dick*, I think, making myself blush.

A broad smile spreads across his handsome face. He licks

his lips in a decidedly sexual way, sending warmth oozing into my crotch. I quickly look down at my hands again, my heart racing. *Holy crap.*

CHAPTER THREE

Dimitri returns from talking to some people on the other side of the room. He's carrying red Solo cups for himself and Clarissa and a bottle of water for me. We girls thank him profusely for his thoughtfulness.

"My pleasure," Dimitri says, tipping his invisible cap to us. "At your service."

I lean in to Clarissa. "He's a cutie. Are you feeling romance or friend zone?"

"I'm not sure yet. I've never had sex with anyone other than an alpha-type before. But I must admit I'm a little curious to see if the rumors are true."

"Rumors?"

"That nerds make it all about *you*."

We both giggle.

"Huh?" Dimitri asks. "What'd I miss?"

"Just a little girl talk," Clarissa says breezily. She pats Dimitri's arm. "Trust me, you'd like it."

Dimitri smiles.

"So, hey, Dimitri, do you know who that dude is with the dark hair and tattoos?" Clarissa asks, motioning toward the keg with her cup. "He was ogling Zooey a few minutes ago."

Dimitri glances across the room toward the keg. "Tyler

Caldwell," he says without hesitation. "Junior. Safety. All-American."

"Free or strong safety?" I ask.

"Oh, you know football?"

I nod. "My dad played in college."

Dimitri nods his approval. "Free. And he's a beast."

"Yeah, I figured he's *somebody*," I say. "Everyone keeps fawning all over him."

"People treat Tyler like he's king of the world any given day, but tonight especially. He had a fumble recovery and two picks in last night's game, including a pick to clinch the win at the very end. It was unbelievable."

I gaze covertly across the room at Tyler. "Based on his shirt, he obviously thinks quite highly of himself."

"Tyler always wears shirts like that. Honestly, I'm not sure if he's serious or trying to be funny. I've never talked to him. But from what I hear, he's an egomaniac. The anti-Jake." He chuckles. "Seriously, you might want to pick another guy to flirt with, Zooey—unless, of course, your goal for the night is to become yet another of Tyler Caldwell's notoriously long list of conquests."

Clarissa and I simultaneously look at each other like "Bingo!" Which, of course, makes us both burst out laughing.

Dimitri chuckles with us, clearly misunderstanding the reason for our laughter. "I mean, I get why girls are attracted to Tyler. He's a huge winner in the DNA lottery, obviously, and he's a beast on the field. Arguably the best safety in the country right now. I can't fathom how he won't be a first-round pick in the draft in the spring. And that means he'll likely be a very wealthy dude one day soon. But, still, even so, it amazes me how girls throw themselves at Tyler and guys like him, even though they know for a fact those kinds of guys aren't even remotely interested in anything beyond..."

I tune Dimitri out again. *Know your audience, dude.*

I glance toward the keg again, and, much to my sizzling delight, Tyler Caldwell's looking straight at me again, his blue eyes on fire. And this time, I don't feel the impulse to look away. *You want to make me another conquest on your notoriously long list, Tyler Caldwell? Well, come and get it, stud.*

Okay, yeah, I'm totally channeling Hot Sandy from *Grease* right now. But it can't be helped. I don't have any other template for how to conduct myself in a situation such as this. Continuing to maintain eye contact with Tyler, I bite my lip, the same way Olivia Newton-John did when she wore that black tight-fitting outfit for John Travolta. *Come and get it, stud.*

Tyler nods subtly like he's heard my exact thoughts.

I flash Tyler a smile that tells him I'm not going to play hard to get tonight, and he beams a gorgeous smile that makes my skin tingle.

So that's it. We're doing this. He knows it. I know it. *It's on.*

Tyler's body language suggests he's saying a quick *adios* to his friends. He takes two loping steps in my direction...just as a stunningly beautiful girl with smooth black hair and porcelain skin appears out of nowhere to throw her arms around his neck. *No!* The girl leans in to whisper something into Tyler's ear. Giggles. Presses herself into his muscled arm. *Crap!*

I look away, my stomach revolting. *Damn, damn, damn!*

Well, that'll teach me to wait so long to give a notorious womanizer my "Hot Sandy Eyes." *Stupid, Zooey!* I tune back in to Dimitri and Clarissa's conversation, forcing myself not to peek at Tyler and that gorgeous girl again, even though that's all I want to do.

"...and she said Tyler didn't even *pretend* to want her phone number," Dimitri is saying.

"Sorry, what? Huh?" I blurt. "I missed the first part of that. Who said what now?"

"My sister's roommate," Dimitri replies. "She slept with Tyler last year, and she said he didn't even *pretend* to want her phone number afterwards." He rolls his eyes with obvious disdain. "Apparently, he told her right up front he couldn't afford any 'emotional distractions' during football season—that football is his only girlfriend at this stage in his life." He scoffs. "I mean, points for honesty, I guess. If he doesn't want a relationship, then it's good he doesn't lead girls on. But, still, I think it's a bit hypocritical for a dude to use football to get girls and then turn around and use football as an excuse to—"

Dimitri abruptly smashes his lips together. His eyes are trained on a target over my left shoulder. I turn and follow Dimitri's wide-eyed gaze...and...promptly lose my shit.

"Hey," Tyler Caldwell says to me, smiling. His voice is deep and smooth, exactly as I'd have expected it to be. He smells faintly of cologne. Maybe whiskey, too? His eyes are savagely blue. He's so damned beautiful, it's like he's got a bright halo of light wafting off him. He puts his hand out. "I'm Tyler Caldwell."

I slide my palm into Tyler's. "Hi there. I'm...hi. Hello."

Clarissa laughs. "She's Zooey. I'm Clarissa, and this is Dimitri."

"What's up, guys?" Tyler says to Clarissa and Dimitri, his hand still holding mine. He addresses Dimitri. "You tutor Jake, right?" He lets go of my hand, much to my chagrin.

"Yeah," Dimitri replies. "And Brayden and Hanalei and Luis, too. But I work the most with Jake."

"You got room for one more?" Tyler asks. "I might need some help this quarter with a bitch of an econ class."

"Sure. No problem."

"Cool. I'll get your number from Hanalei." Tyler's eyes return to me. He slides his hand into mine again. "Sorry about that. I didn't come over here to get myself a tutor—I came over here to introduce myself to the beautiful girl who's making it impossible for me to concentrate on a damned thing anybody's saying to me."

I open and close my mouth like a fish on a line. And that's all I can muster.

"So..." Tyler says, filling the awkward silence. "How come I've never seen you at one of our parties before? I'm positive I would have remembered you."

Clarissa nudges me.

"Oh, this is *your* party?" I blurt.

"Well, mine and my roommates'. I live here with five of my teammates."

I take a steadying breath. Clear my throat. "Cool. I live in the dorms. Hendrick Hall." I point at Clarissa. "With her."

Tyler looks like he's just bitten into a lemon. "You're a freshman?"

I nod. "A theater major."

He sighs. "Please at least tell me you're eighteen. If you're jail bait, I swear to God I'm going to sob into my pillow tonight."

My clit is tingling. My skin is buzzing. I've never felt so physically attracted to another human being in all my life. "No sobbing necessary. I turned eighteen in July."

Tyler wipes his brow comically. "Thank God." His eyes sweep down my body and back up again. "I don't typically go for freshman, but if ever there was a reason to break my cardinal rule, it's you."

I screw up my face. "Thank you?"

"It's a compliment."

"Why don't you typically 'go for freshman'?"

"Because, no offense, half the time it turns out they're batshit crazy."

I shoot him a snarky look.

"Sorry, but it's true."

"So let me get this straight. Batshit crazy freshman girls magically transform into perfectly sane ones at the start of their second year?"

He laughs. "Well, it sounds kind of stupid when you put it like that. I think what I'm trying to say is that some people, both guys and girls, need that first year of being away from home to get their batshit crazy out of their systems. Freshman girls in particular seem to have a harder time than anyone else grasping the concept that having a little fun with someone isn't the same thing as finding a soulmate."

I look at Clarissa, intending to flash her a look that says, *Ding, ding, ding! We've found ourselves a cherry-popper, folks!*

But she's engaged in a conversation with Dimitri. "Well, let me assure you," I say to Tyler. "I'm not looking for my soulmate. And even if I were, which I'm *not*, I'm quite certain he wouldn't be caught dead in a T-shirt that says God's Gift to Womankind."

Tyler chuckles. "Touché, little freshman."

"How old are you, Tyler?" I ask.

"I just turned twenty-one."

"Uh oh. I don't normally go for guys under twenty-two. Batshit crazy, all of them."

He grins.

"But I suppose if ever there was a reason to break my cardinal rule, it'd be you."

Tyler bites his lower lip. "Lucky me."

I smile coyly. "*Very* lucky you." *Holy shit! Who am I right now?*

Tyler and I stare at each other for a long moment, the heat between us palpable. During the stillness between us, the song in the living room switches from a hip-hop thumper to a slow and sexy R&B groove.

Tyler doesn't miss a beat. He leans right in to my ear. "Dance with me."

Heat flashes onto my cheeks. I nod.

And that's that. Tyler grabs my hand and leads me through the crowded kitchen like a medieval groom pulling his virgin bride to their marital bed. And just that fast, I can see my future in Tyler Caldwell's delectable ass as he leads me toward the dance floor, as surely as if I were looking into a very muscular crystal ball. I'm going to lose my virginity tonight to God's Gift to Womankind. *And it's going to be oh-so good.*

CHAPTER FOUR

Once Tyler has found his preferred spot in the middle of the packed dance floor, he turns around, wraps his muscled arms loosely around me, and begins moving his insanely fit body to the slow and sensuous beat of the R&B groove. In reply, I slide my arms around Tyler's neck and begin moving my body in synchronicity with his, letting my breasts brush lightly against his hard chest as I gyrate.

At my receptive body language, Tyler pulls me toward him, ever so slightly, apparently testing my boundaries. *All righty, then.* Time to make my lack of boundaries abundantly clear. I move closer to Tyler and brush my crotch lightly against his as I move to the beat of the music...and, almost instantaneously, I'm rewarded with the sensation of a hard-on rising up and nudging against my crotch. My breath hitches. My skin sizzles and pops. *Delicious.*

Tyler leans in to my ear. "You're so hot," he says, his breath warm against my skin.

My body explodes with excitement. "So are you."

"I love the dress."

"Thank you."

But I'm not here to talk. I tighten my arms around his neck and grind my aching clit against his hard-on like a mewing cat on a scratching pole. It's something I've been dreaming of doing with a hot guy for the better part of a year, and I'm not holding back. I must say, the reality of doing this *far* exceeds my fantasy of it. I grind harder, thinly disguising my movement as dancing, and Tyler responds in kind, thrusting his erection against my epicenter.

"Oh, Jesus," I blurt, my body exploding into flames of desire.

Without hesitation, he lifts my thigh around his waist, a maneuver that opens my crotch to him like a blooming flower, and presses his hard-on against me with sniper-like precision.

I groan loudly at the incredible sensation, but, thank God, the embarrassing sound is swallowed by the loud music.

Tyler leans in to my ear. "Can I grab your ass?"

I nod.

Without hesitation, he cups my ass cheek in his large palm, pulling my body even more fiercely into his massive bulge. His lips brush my face and land on my ear. "I don't want a relationship," he breathes.

Boom. There it is. Exactly what Dimitri warned me was coming. "Neither do I," I say into his ear. "Just...oh, God. Please don't stop what you're doing."

Tyler's lips leave my ear and brush gently against my cheek...and then make their way to my lips. His mouth skims mine softly. Briefly. And then again. Clearly, he's asking for permission to kiss me. So I give it to him. I lean forward and brush my lips against his, making it clear I want him to go in for the kill. So he does. He opens my lips with his and slides his tongue into my mouth and, just like that, I'm a goner. *Oh, God, it's official.* I want to have sex with this human.

We're both on fire. Not even pretending to dance anymore. Kissing without inhibition. Dry-humping in the middle of the packed dance floor. Groaning into each other's mouths while our hands furiously grope and grab. The pleasure I'm feeling is so intense, so shockingly sublime, I feel like I'm losing control of my limbs. I *grind* even more desperately into his hardness, kissing him furiously and quaking with arousal.

A faint fluttering announces itself between my legs, making me moan. I smash my body into Tyler's and devour his lips even more fervently, grinding my crotch into his hard bulge like my life depends on it. Oh, God, I'm ramping up in ways I've never experienced before. Aroused and excited and swollen in a whole new, desperate way.

Someone behind me on the packed dance floor laughs sharply. And then I'm jostled on the shoulder. Another laugh. And just like that, the spell is broken. That warping I'm beginning to feel deep inside my core abruptly stops. I slide my thigh down and yank my crotch away from Tyler's, suddenly ashamed of myself. I can't believe I've been attacking this boy so brazenly in plain sight of everyone at this party. I can't imagine what people must be thinking of me.

Tyler puts his palm on my cheek and his forehead against mine. "I want you," he says simply.

I inhale his scent and my entire body melts into him. "I want you, too," I reply honestly.

Tyler grins wickedly. "My bedroom's upstairs."

I nod. "Let's go."

CHAPTER FIVE

Tyler leads me up a staircase. My heart is racing. My crotch is throbbing. When we reach the middle of the stairs, a new song begins blaring from below in the living room. Pitbull's "Come & Go"—a song about Pitbull's self-proclaimed talent for bringing women to climax.

"Hey, they're playing my song," Tyler says playfully.

"God, I hope so," I mutter. "Fingers crossed."

"No need to cross a thing, pretty girl," Tyler says. "Fingers, legs, or otherwise. I guarantee you'll get off harder with me than ever before."

I snort. "Well, if I get off *once* it'll be..." I abruptly smash my lips together. What the fuckity am I doing? *Now is not the time to nervously reveal your secrets, Zooey!* But it's too late. Tyler abruptly stops ascending the staircase, his body language making it clear he's understood my meaning.

"You've never had an orgasm?" he asks.

I release Tyler's hand, feeling self-conscious, but remain silent.

"Don't be embarrassed about it," he says soothingly. "You've obviously been with nothing but idiots and selfish bastards." He smiles, takes my hand, and begins leading me up the stairs again. "Don't you worry, sweetheart. I'll make sure you cross the finish line quicker than Usain Bolt."

Relief floods me. "Oh, thank you," I say lamely, like he's offered to change my flat tire.

"In fact, I'll make sure you cross it more than once."

I'm absolutely giddy. "Well, twice would be a nice bonus. But do it *once* and you'll rock my world. I've been *dying* to finally know what it feels like."

Tyler stops walking again. We're now at the end of a hallway, standing outside a closed door. "Wait. You've never had an orgasm, *ever*? I thought you meant you haven't had one *with a guy*."

Crap. What the heck have I done? Not once when I've fantasized about finding a hot stranger to pop my cherry did I imagine myself having this conversation with him beforehand. *Stupid, stupid, Zooey!* "I haven't had one at all," I admit, my face bursting into flames.

"But..." All of a sudden, complete understanding visibly washes over Tyler's handsome features. "You're a *virgin*?"

There's a burst of female laughter on the staircase behind us, followed by a low male voice.

"Can we talk about this somewhere else, please?" I snap.

Tyler grabs my hand and leads me through a nearby door. "You're a *virgin*?" he repeats as he shuts the door behind us.

I smash my lips together, pissed at myself. I've always instinctively known revealing my virginal status before doing the deed with a stranger would lead to nothing good. Performance anxiety for the guy, perhaps? Or maybe my designated cherry-popper would turn out to be a virgin-fetishist who'd be a bit *too* excited to go where no man has gone before? I glance around the room, feeling like a trapped animal. My panicked eyes flicker across the posters on Tyler's walls. Muhammad Ali. Usain Bolt. Some football player in a Broncos uniform. A poster of "The Four Greatest Michaels of All Time."

"Zooey?" Tyler says, drawing my anxious gaze away from the posters and back to him. "I'm not judging you. I'm trying to understand the situation so I don't mess this up for you. It's kind of a big deal."

I smash my lips together even tighter.

"You're a virgin?" he asks a third time.

I exhale. "Yes."

Tyler runs his hand through his hair. "But...are you a 'Catholic Virgin'? You know, you've done everything there is to do besides actual intercourse?"

My cheeks feel hot. "No. I've done nothing but kissing and basic making out."

Tyler looks positively blown away. "No one's ever gone down on you?"

My chest feels tight. "I don't feel comfortable talking about this. You'll notice I'm not asking you about *your* sexual experience."

"I wouldn't normally ask, but this is a once-in-a-lifetime thing for you. No do-overs." He furrows his brow. "I can't believe you were going to let me have sex with you without bothering to mention you're a virgin."

"What difference does it make? Just do whatever you were planning to do before you found out. I'm sure it'll be fantabulous for us both."

He scowls. "Zooey, letting some random, drunk-ass dude at a party take your virginity, without even bothering to tell him the situation, wouldn't have been 'fantabulous' for you. You're lucky you got me, but you were playing Russian roulette. What were you thinking?"

Okay, now I'm not only feeling embarrassed but pissed, too. "So I'm getting slut-shamed by a guy wearing a God's Gift to Womankind T-shirt? Is that what's happening here?"

Tyler rolls his eyes. "The word 'slut' isn't even in my vocabulary. I'm just thrown for a loop. We practically fucked each other down there on the dance floor and now I find out..." He sighs. "Look, this isn't about me, okay? I just don't want to fuck this up for you. The first time's a big deal. You'll remember it forever."

"It doesn't have to be a big deal. In fact, that's my whole point. I've decided not to buy into all the pressure and hype about losing my virginity. I've decided it's *not* a big deal."

Tyler scoffs. "I don't think you get to decide that. Whether you like it or not, this is going to be a lifelong memory for you. Not to mention, if I'm being honest, I'm worried you're going to get weirdly attached to me afterwards. Turn into a Stage Five Clinger. Slash my tires. Light up my phone."

"I thought this wasn't about you."

"Yeah, well, I guess it is. It takes two to tango, after all."

I roll my eyes. "I won't get 'weirdly attached' to you, Tyler. After you relieve me of my virginity, I promise I'll never want to see you again."

Tyler looks utterly unconvinced.

I cross my arms over my chest. "You were perfectly

willing to screw me a minute ago when you thought I had lots of experience. So what's the difference?"

He rolls his entire head, not just his eyes. "You *really* don't know what you don't know. Your first time, the guy needs to be extra gentle. He needs to talk you through it and make sure you're okay every step of the way. He shouldn't be some drunk-ass guy at a party who has no idea it's your first time. For God's sake, Zooey, at the very least, find yourself some nice guy who'll buy you a fucking cheeseburger beforehand and then be sober enough to drive you safely home afterwards. *Jesus.*"

I clench my jaw. "Was *your* first time some sort of beautiful, poignant experience preceded by cheeseburgers?" I ask caustically.

"Yeah, it was, actually," he replies. "It was beautiful and poignant and poetic."

I feel myself blush. "*Oh.*"

Tyler snorts. "Just kidding. It was completely meaningless. My best friend's stepsister's cousin. I don't even remember her name." He snorts again. "But that's why I know for a fact you don't want to do it that way. I'm a *dude* and, afterwards, even *I* felt a little bit like I should have waited and done things differently for my first time. I can't even imagine how I would have felt if I'd been a girl and done it that same way."

I put my hands on my hips. "*If you'd been a girl?* Do you have any idea how sexist a comment that was?"

"*Sexist?* How the hell am I being sexist? All I want to do is fuck you right now—that's *all* I want to do. And yet, despite how badly I want to do that, I'm respecting you enough to protect you from doing something you'll more than likely regret. How the fuck is that *sexist*?"

"Because your 'respect' and 'protection' are completely paternalistic."

"*Paternalistic?*"

"It means—"

"I know what it means. I might be a football player, but I'm not a dumb jock."

"I don't think you're dumb, Tyler, but you're obviously stupid about this. You wouldn't give this same advice to a *guy*. And you know why? Because guys are *studs* if they lose their virginity to a hot stranger at a party. Just look at all the movies about that very thing. *Superbad. Risky Business. American Pie.* I could go on and on. And nobody ever says, 'Oh dear, that nice young man really should have waited to make sure his first time was with someone who'd buy him a freaking cheeseburger beforehand!'"

Tyler makes a face like he's utterly annoyed.

I pull a rolling chair out from a small desk in the corner, kick off my heels, and plop myself down. "Look, Mr. God's Gift, here's the thing. I didn't come to this party dressed like this to get lectured by some football player in a douchey shirt about the sanctity of my virginity or to debate society's double standards about male and female sexuality. I came out tonight to find a guy exactly like you to have sex with and, in the process, hopefully get to have my first orgasm. It's as simple as that."

"A guy like me?"

I motion to his shirt. "A guy who's clearly not boyfriend material."

"Why am I not boyfriend material?"

"Are you joking? Tyler, you said so yourself!"

He moves to the foot of his bed and sits. "No, what I said was I'm not looking for a relationship. That doesn't mean I don't consider myself boyfriend *material*. What *I* said reflects my relationship status by choice. What *you* said is an assault on my very character."

"Oh, come on, Tyler. You can't wear a shirt like that and then get offended when I say you're not boyfriend material."

He still looks offended. "I'd make an amazing boyfriend if I wanted to be one. Which I *don't* at the present time. But if I *did*, I'd be amazing and any girl would be lucky to have me. I'm loyal. Faithful. Thoughtful. Funny. Great in bed. Not sure what makes a guy 'boyfriend material' if not all that."

"Um, gee, the desire to have a girlfriend?"

He scoffs.

"Surely, other guys on the team have girlfriends," I say.

"Other guys on the team aren't me. They haven't devoted the past nine years of their lives to going top ten in the draft. They aren't entering the draft at the end of their junior year because they're already one of the hottest commodities in the country." He clenches his jaw. "They're not so close to the Promised Land they can *taste* it."

Tyler's intensity silences me for a long moment. My heart is thudding in my ears. Damn, he's a sexy dude. Finally, I venture, "Dimitri said the quarterback had a girlfriend until recently. Is he not trying to go top ten in the draft?"

Tyler shakes his head. "Jake's not entering the draft until next year," he says. "And when he does, he'll be lucky if he goes in the second round. He's perfect for our offensive scheme, but he's a system quarterback, not a true pro prospect. But, regardless, Jake's just a different species of human than me. Actually, I'm not even sure Jake's human. He's got ice in his veins, that guy, both on and off the field. Nothing affects him."

"And you?"

"I'm the anti-Jake. *Everything* affects me. I'm passionate. If I had a girlfriend, I'd worry about her. If someone were to act like an asshole to her, I'd be ready to rip the guy's head off. If my girlfriend and I had a fight before a game, then I'd play like shit that day. And I can't risk any of that."

I stare at him for a moment, my crotch suddenly tingling. Is it weird everything he just said turned me on? "Okay, Tyler, fine. I'm willing to concede you'd be boyfriend material *if* that's what you wanted to be."

"Thank you."

"But I won't back down from saying your shirt gives the exact opposite impression."

"Yeah, well, maybe that's part of my reason for wearing the shirt." He taps his temple and winks.

"Wow. So you're saying the douchey shirt is some sort of secret code? Like, it wards off girls looking for a boyfriend?"

"Something like that."

"And here I thought *you* thought your shirt was nothing but a simple statement of fact."

"Oh, I do. Definitely. Plus—bonus points—it's funny as hell."

"How can your shirt be a simple statement of fact *and* funny as hell at the same time? You're either serious or joking.

It can't be both."

Tyler smiles. "Sure it can."

"I don't see how."

"If you saw an elephant wearing a T-shirt with the word elephant stamped across it, you'd think that's pretty damned funny, right?"

I can't help smiling. *Ah, so he's more clever than I gave him credit for.* "That depends."

"Aw, come on," he says, flashing me a snarky look. "Don't argue with me for the sake of arguing."

"I'm not. An elephant in an elephant T-shirt *might* be funny and it might not."

"Tell me one scenario where an elephant wearing an elephant T-shirt wouldn't be fucking hilarious."

I slide my legs underneath me in the chair, taking care not to flash Tyler my undies as I do. I say, "Well, if the elephant was harmed or humiliated while being stuffed into his elephant T-shirt, that wouldn't be funny. Animal cruelty is never a laughing matter, Tyler Caldwell."

Tyler chuckles. "The elephant wasn't harmed or humiliated."

"How can you be sure? Elephants are highly intelligent creatures. It's well known they experience complex emotions."

"I know because he's a *cartoon* elephant."

Again, I can't resist smiling broadly. "Ah, so our elephant is like Babar, is he?"

"*Babar?* Who's that?"

"You don't know Babar?"

Tyler shakes his head. He's got an adorable, crooked grin

on his face. "Is he a cartoon elephant?"

I'm aghast. "How do you not know Babar? Did you grow up under a rock?"

"Lots of different rocks. We moved around a lot when I was a kid."

"Military?"

"Football. My dad played in the NFL for nine seasons. But he wasn't a superstar, so he never had job security. A season here. A season there. We moved every time he got picked up by a new team."

"What position did he play?"

"You know football?"

"I was raised on it. My dad played for the University of Nebraska."

"Ah, a Cornhusker. What position?"

"Center."

"Did he go pro?"

"He tried, but he never made it onto a roster. Too small. What was your dad's position?"

"Defensive tackle."

"Which teams?"

Tyler tells me a long string of team names, ending with the Dallas Cowboys.

"Your dad must be thrilled you're following in his footsteps. Did he want you to be a defensive tackle, too?"

"No, he wanted me to be a quarterback, actually. I tried when I was younger, but it turns out my throwing arm is a cannon with zero accuracy. But, hey, consolation prize, the free safety is known as the 'quarterback of the defense.'"

"Why is that?"

"I make the coverage call and communicate it to the linebackers and other DBs. I disguise the look. Check the defense and make sure everyone adjusts and gets into position." Tyler taps his temple. "I use my brain as much as my body out there, sweetheart. That's why I love the position so much."

My skin is buzzing. Tyler comes alive when he talks about football, and it's incredibly sexy.

"Hey, you want a water?" Tyler asks.

"Sure. Thanks."

He gets up and grabs two bottles from a mini-fridge in the corner, hands one to me, and then leans on the edge of his desk a foot away from me, twisting the cap on his bottle. "So tell me about this Babar dude," Tyler says, his blue eyes blazing. "He's a cartoon elephant in a T-shirt?"

"No, he's a cartoon elephant in a snazzy green suit and a yellow crown."

"Then it sounds like the better choice for our cartoon elephant's doppelgänger would be Winnie the Pooh."

I make a face like that's the dumbest thing I've ever heard. "Why on earth would our cartoon elephant's doppelgänger be a cartoon *bear*?"

"Because Winnie the Pooh wears a T-shirt, not a snazzy green suit and a crown."

I make a buzzing sound. "Thanks for playing, but Pooh wears a *polo* shirt."

"*No.* Pooh wears a red T-shirt. I've seen it a million times."

"Pooh's shirt has a collar on it. That makes it a *polo* shirt."

"Jesus God, I've brought a madwoman into my bedroom.

Please don't hurt me." He pulls out his phone. "Prepare to be schooled, Zooey... What's your last name?"

"Cartwright."

"Prepare to be schooled, Zooey Cartwright. I'm one hundred percent—" He gasps. "Holy shit! Winnie the Pooh wears a red *polo* shirt!"

"I guess I should have warned you. I only argue when I'm sure I'm right."

Tyler looks at his phone again. "I'm deeply traumatized."

"That's nothing. If you *really* want to be traumatized, then consider this: *Why the hell isn't Pooh wearing pants?* He's a bear who lives in a house and sleeps in a bed. He drinks tea out of a cup. And yet he wears no pants with his polo shirt? I mean, is Pooh fully anthropomorphized or not? Because, if he is, then he's a 'public lewdness' charge waiting to happen."

Tyler throws his head back and laughs heartily...and the sound of his full-throated laughter sends pangs of regret shooting through my chest. *Damn it.* He's so freaking adorable. And witty. And hot. He's so much more than I thought he'd be when I first laid eyes on him. Why'd I have to throw myself at him, dressed like this? Why couldn't I have met him on campus while looking and acting like myself? Why couldn't we have struck up a conversation in the book store—the same way Dimitri and Clarissa did? If only I could rewind time and—

Wait.

What on earth is my crazy brain thinking? Wishing I'd met Tyler under different circumstances is a pointless exercise because Tyler doesn't want a girlfriend. And I most certainly don't want a boyfriend. To the contrary, now that I'm finally out from under my father's protective thumb, I'm determined to have nothing but fun, fun, fun throughout my entire freshman year.

Tyler wipes his eyes from laughing. "Wow. Thanks for fucking up *Winnie the Pooh* for me."

"Misery loves company."

Tyler flashes me a smile that sends butterflies shooting into my stomach. "Okay. That was a nice deflection, but it's time for you to give me your final answer." He puts his water bottle down and crosses his muscled arms over his chest. "*Time's up, Zooey.*"

CHAPTER SIX

I stare at Tyler blankly, not sure what he means. He needs my final answer about what? If I'm willing to have sex with him, after all? Because, if so, my answer would most definitely be... *yes*.

"Do you admit our cartoon elephant's T-shirt is funny or not?" Tyler demands. "Assuming, *of course*, he's wearing pants."

Oh. That. "Um..." I begin but trail off. My mind is racing. I think I might have royally screwed up tonight. Tyler's clearly not the douchebag I thought he was based on initial impressions. Not at all. He's actually someone I'd love to hang out with and get to know. Which means the fact that I threw myself at him... *and then got turned down*...is absolutely mortifying. I clear my throat. "I can't give you my final answer yet," I say. I lean back in my chair. "There are still too many variables."

"*Variables?* Well, this I've got to hear." Tyler shifts his backside against the edge of his desk like he's settling in for the night and flashes me a smile that says *Enlighten me*.

"Well, for one thing," I say. "I'd want to know if our cartoon elephant *chose* his elephant T-shirt out of his cartoon closet the same way a human hipster would choose a T-shirt that says Human."

Tyler chuckles. "Or..."

"*Or*, in the alternative, if the word elephant on the elephant's T-shirt is completely outside the realm of his cartoon reality."

"Outside the realm of his cartoon reality?" Tyler chuckles, and his stunningly blue eyes twinkle at me.

I clear my throat again. Oh, man, my insides suddenly feel like an ice cream cone left out on a sunny day. "Yeah, you know, like, maybe the word elephant on his T-shirt is actually a label."

"A *label*?"

"Placed on his shirt by the illustrator to make sure we can tell he's an elephant."

Tyler shakes his head like I've given him whiplash. "The elephant is a big gray animal with a trunk and tiny tail. No label necessary."

"That's your *assumption*. But there are lots of reasons why a label might be necessary."

"Name two," Tyler says.

I take a deep breath, trying to steady my pounding heart. "Well, what if the illustrator is a kindergartner, and the elephant looks like nothing but a big gray blob?"

Tyler chuckles.

"Or what if the illustrator is some old guy who's recently had a stroke and, sadly, the elephant looks more like a gigantic boulder with eyes?"

Tyler bites his lower lip. "Or maybe a rhino."

"*Exactly*. See? Now you get it. Surely, in either of those scenarios, a label on the elephant would be necessary—and not the least bit funny."

Tyler bites his lip again and then shoots me a smoldering look that hardens my nipples. "The elephant is a hipster, Zooey," he says evenly, his eyes locked with mine. "He got his elephant T-shirt at a vintage shop, and he drinks old fashioneds at elephant bars while listening to cartoon bands you've never heard of."

"Ah, so our cartoon elephant must not listen to Josie and the Pussycats, then. They'd be way too mainstream for his hipster musical taste." I snort at my own joke, but the look on Tyler's face tells me he has no idea what I'm talking about. "Aw, come on, man!" I bellow. "First Babar and now Josie and the Pussycats?"

Tyler shrugs.

"Damn. And that was a clever joke, too. Trust me, if you'd grown up watching Cartoon Network on Saturdays like me, rather than wasting your time and energy playing football all the time, you'd understand that joke absolutely slayed."

"Oh, I'm sure it did. There's no doubt in my mind." His eyes flicker with heat. "Okay, Zooey. Are there any more *variables* you need to consider or are you finally ready to concede the point?"

"What's the point again?"

He rolls his eyes. "That the elephant's T-shirt, and therefore mine, can be both a statement of fact *and* funny."

I bite the inside of my cheek. Exhale. And finally, begrudgingly, motion to his T-shirt and say, "Fine. I concede. It's a damned funny shirt."

Tyler fist-pumps the air, throws his head back, and lets out a laugh that's so adorable, it makes my crotch flutter. And just like that, another pang of regret shoots through me. I can't believe I threw myself at this gorgeous guy...*and he turned me down*. Suddenly, I want to bolt out of this bedroom and never look back.

I rise out of my chair and put my water bottle down. "So, hey, Mr. God's Gift to Womankind, it's been great meeting you, but I think I'm going to head downstairs, find my roommate, and go back to the dorms now."

Tyler's face falls. "Is something wrong?"

"I'm just tired." *And embarrassed.* "Have a great rest of your season and good luck in the draft in May."

I begin crossing the room, intending to flee, but Tyler beats me to the door and stands in front of it. "Hang on. Something's obviously wrong."

"Nope. Nothing's wrong. I've just realized you're totally right. It was a huge mistake for me to come up here with you." *And now I'm feeling embarrassed and rejected and mortified about it.* "Honestly, I'd like to leave and forget tonight ever happened."

"Shit." He exhales. "Zooey, listen. All that stuff I said earlier, I'm thinking maybe I jumped the gun and we should—"

"No, no, you were absolutely right. I would have regretted having a one-night stand with you. I might even have turned into a Stage Five Clinger on you, to be honest. You know how freshman girls are—we're all batshit crazy, especially small-town girls like me with no experience." I force a smile. "Truthfully, I think we both dodged huge bullets tonight. I dodged giving my V card to some random, drunk-ass dude at a party who didn't even buy me a freaking cheeseburger first.

And you dodged having a potential Stage Five Clinger on your hands." I force another smile, even though my stomach is suddenly churning. "So let's both count our lucky stars and call it a night." I motion for him to step away from the door. "Excuse me, please."

Tyler sighs and slowly steps aside, a pained expression on his face. "*Shit*," he mutters. "Zooey, listen—"

"No, no. Please. There's nothing more to say. Have fun avoiding 'emotional distractions' until the draft." With that, I swing open Tyler's bedroom door and bolt down the hallway, praying to God I'll never see Tyler Caldwell and his savagely blue eyes and heart-stopping smile ever again.

CHAPTER SEVEN

I stop walking and look down at the campus map on my phone, trying in vain to figure out how to get to Randolph Hall. This is my first time down here in South Campus, the land of future scientists, and this map isn't helping me at all. Thank God I came down south with so much extra time before the start of my Social Psychology class, or I'd be totally stressed right now. I look up from my phone, trying to orient myself, and immediately notice Dimitri walking about twenty yards away.

"Dimitri!" I call out.

Dimitri stops and looks straight at me, not a hint of recognition on his face, and then continues on his merry way as if I've said nothing at all.

"Dimitri!" I shout again, bounding toward him. I wave at him like a dork. "It's Zooey from the football party!"

Dimitri's eyes widen with astonishment. "Holy crap, I didn't even recognize you!" He embraces me, laughing. "You look so different with your hair curly like this. I *love* it."

I touch my crazy hair. "Yeah, Clarissa gave me quite the makeover the other night." I motion to my tank top, shorts, and sneakers. "The real Zooey is more Farm Girl from Nebraska than Kendall Jenner."

"You look awesome either way." He shifts his backpack on his shoulder. "So how's Clarissa? We're meeting tomorrow for coffee. Got any pro tips for me?"

"Pro tips?"

"Inside info I can use to make her fall desperately in love with me."

I make an "aw" face. "Just be your sweet and charming self, Dimitri. After the party, Clarissa said some really nice things about you."

"'Nice' as in 'he's totally in my friend zone,' or...?" Dimitri looks at me expectantly, obviously hoping I'll spill the beans. But I've got nothing for him. After the party, Clarissa and I stayed up talking for hours and hours, at which time she told me she likes Dimitri a lot, but she's on the fence about whether she could see herself sleeping with him. "He's definitely cute," she said that night. "But he didn't even try to kiss me, even though I kept giving him green-light signals. If a guy doesn't make a move on me early on, the window for romance slams shut. It's just the way I'm wired. I need to feel desirable right away."

I look into Dimitri's earnest, expectant face, and my heart pangs for him. "Okay, Dimitri, I've got one pro tip for you. You've got to cowboy up and make your move early with Clarissa. If you don't make her feel like she's completely irresistible to you, she'll put you in the friend zone, and that will be that. No second chances."

Dimitri looks distressed.

"Just go for it," I urge. "Better to make a move and get rejected than wonder 'what if' later on."

Dimitri takes a deep breath. "Wow, thanks, Zooey. Okay, I'll go for it."

"Good luck."

"So enough about me and my whopping crush on your unbelievably gorgeous roommate who totally rocked my world the other night," Dimitri says. "How's your first day of classes treating you so far, college girl?"

"So far, so good. I had History of Theater this morning up in my neck of the woods. And now I'm down south to take my required science class. *Shudder.*"

"What class?"

"Social Psychology. Thankfully, I'll be heading back up north immediately afterwards for Modernizing Shakespeare."

"Oh, I took that class last quarter for my creative writing minor. It was cool."

"Awesome. So would you mind giving me directions to Randolph? I'm terrible at reading maps, and I don't want to be late for class."

"It's not you, it's the map. The first time I tried to find Randolph my freshman year, I got lost for four days. If I hadn't had a granola bar and a Red Bull in my backpack, I would have starved to death while waiting for the search party." He grins adorably. "I'll walk you there. It'll give me a chance to tell you about an interesting text I got from a certain someone right after the party."

The hair on the back of my neck stands up. "Who?"

"Tyler Caldwell."

Oh, jeez. If Tyler told Dimitri what happened between us—and the secrets I told him—I'll freaking kill him. "A text from Tyler Caldwell?" I choke out. "About what?"

"He wanted to know if I happened to have Clarissa's phone number so he could get—"

"Dimitri!" a male voice booms a few feet to our right, and we both look toward the sound.

Oh, for the love of all things embarrassing and mortifying! *No.* It's none other than God's Gift to Womankind loping toward us! Where's a girl's invisibility cloak when she needs one? But there's nowhere to hide. Tyler is jogging straight toward Dimitri, his stunningly perfect body poetry in motion, the phrase You're Welcome! plastered in white letters across his black T-shirt.

My brain is screaming at me to flee. And yet, I can't move a muscle.

Oh, lord. Seeing Tyler today, I'm feeling every bit as attracted to him as I did the other night. More so, actually. As he moves so effortlessly toward us in the glorious California sunshine, his muscles flexing and bulging, he's more Superman than Loki. And I must admit I've always had a thing for Superman.

"Hey," Tyler says to Dimitri, coming to a stand next to me.

Without consciously meaning to do it, I quickly take two lurching steps backward until I'm standing two feet behind Tyler's broad shoulder.

"Hey, Tyler," Dimitri says. "What a coincidence. I got your text and, now, *voila.*" He motions over Tyler's shoulder toward me, but Tyler doesn't turn around. To the contrary, Tyler remains focused on Dimitri's face like a sniper peering through his scope.

"Did you hear back from her roommate yet?" Tyler asks urgently.

My skin pricks. *Am I the "her" in that sentence?*

Dimitri looks at me over Tyler's shoulder again and grins. "I haven't texted Clarissa yet. I'm meeting her for coffee tomorrow, so I figured I'd ask her for Zooey's number then. But now that Zooey happens to be—"

"*Tomorrow?*" Tyler booms. "I can't wait that long, man!" He runs his hand through his hair. "Listen, man. You've got to do me a solid and give that roommate of hers a call right now. Let me sweet-talk her into giving me Zooey's number before I lose my mind."

Dimitri flashes Tyler a face that says, *You're the stupidest human alive.* "Hey, Tyler," he says. "You might want to shake your head because I think your eyes are stuck. Oh, and you might want to put on your listening ears, too. What I was *trying* to tell you when you interrupted me is that I was *planning* to ask Clarissa for Zooey's number in person *tomorrow* because, apparently, Zooey left the party the other night not wanting to see you ever again. *But*, as I was further *trying* to tell you, waiting until tomorrow to ask Clarissa for Zooey's number is now a moot point because she's—"

"*A moot point?*" Tyler bellows. "If Zooey left the party never wanting to see me again, that's even more reason why I need her number *now*. God only knows what guys she's been meeting these past two days in her dorms or at the student center or wherever." He grunts like a gorilla. "Look, man, I made a huge mistake with Zooey the other night—an epically huge I'm-a-total-dumbshit mistake—and I haven't stopped regretting it since."

Dimitri bites his lip like he's trying not to burst out laughing. He glances at me behind Tyler's shoulder again, and I shake my head frantically, telling him not to let on that I'm standing here.

Dimitri's gaze returns to Tyler. "Wow, man," Dimitri says. "What on earth did you do to Zooey that's got you so wound up?"

My entire body tenses. *Oh, crap.* Part of me wants to scream, "I'm standing right behind you, Tyler!" to keep Tyler from divulging the mortifying truth about what happened between us. But an even larger part of me desperately wants to hear whatever Tyler's going to reply, no matter how embarrassing it might be.

"The details don't matter," Tyler says, swatting at the air. "Bottom line is that Zooey asked me to...um...grab a cheeseburger with her. And I said no."

My body relaxes. *Thank God.*

"I figured there was no point in me grabbing a cheeseburger with her because it couldn't lead to anything, you know? Football's my focus right now, and a cute girl like her wanting to grab a cheeseburger with me felt kind of like I'd be leading her on. But the minute she left, I realized I'd messed up—that I shouldn't have said no to a simple *cheeseburger.* I mean, if that's what the girl wants, who am I to turn her down? It's just one meal, after all. It doesn't *have* to turn into anything more than that, no matter how hot she is. But now I'm tortured with thoughts of her grabbing a cheeseburger with some other guy." His voice takes on an unmistakable urgency. "So, please, just text Zooey's roommate and get her damned number for me so I can call her and ask her to get a cheeseburger with me as soon as humanly possible."

Dimitri chuckles. "Oh, my God. This is comedy gold. Okay, Tyler, I've had my fun. Turn around. Zooey's standing right behind you." He motions to me. "Literally, right behind you, dude."

Tyler slowly turns around, and his expression morphs into the one every cartoon character makes whenever they see an oncoming locomotive. "*Zooey?*"

I shoot him a clipped wave. "Hi."

Tyler's eyes sweep over my curly hair and makeup-free face and then traverse the full length of my body before locking onto my face again. He swallows hard. "How long have you been standing there?"

I bite my lip. I'm quite certain this is one of the most deliciously satisfying moments of my entire life. And one I intend to milk for all it's worth. "I was talking to Dimitri when you first walked up and interrupted us. I heard every single word you said."

Tyler palms his forehead.

"And while I appreciate everything you told Dimitri—I truly do—I should tell you I've completely changed my mind about grabbing a cheeseburger with you. I mean, don't get me wrong, I do still crave having a cheeseburger with *someone*, but just not with you."

Tyler turns to Dimitri, looking forlorn. "Could you excuse us for a minute, nerd?"

I bristle. *Nerd?* Wow. Just because Tyler's feeling

humiliated in this moment, doesn't mean he can take it out on Dimitri. "Don't go, *Dimitri*," I say, taking special care to emphasize Dimitri's name in light of Tyler's snub. "You promised to walk me to Randolph for my next class, remember, *Dimitri?*"

Tyler's face lights up. "Your next class is in Randolph?"

I nod. "Social Psych in"—I look at my watch—"fifteen minutes. So, unfortunately, I have to get a move-on. Great seeing you again, Tyler. Love the shirt. Good luck avoiding any and all emotional distractions until May." I motion to Dimitri. "Come on, *Dimitri*."

"Hang on, *nerd*," Tyler says sharply. "I'll walk her."

Yet again with the "nerd" thing? What is this, *The Breakfast Club*? "No thank you," I say tightly. "I wouldn't dream of inconveniencing you. Come on, *Dimitri*."

"It'd be no inconvenience at all," Tyler says, a wicked smile spreading across his gorgeous face. "It just so happens my next class is Social Psych in Randolph, too."

CHAPTER EIGHT

"It's true," I say, walking stiffly alongside Tyler through swarms of students. "Thanks to you, I've realized there's a big difference between sexual liberation and sexual stupidity. Plus, truth be told, I'm not physically attracted to you anymore. Not after the way you treated Dimitri back there."

Tyler stops walking, and I follow suit. He looks genuinely baffled. "After the way I treated Dimitri? What are you talking about?"

I roll my eyes. "The fact that you don't even know what dicky thing you did to Dimitri is even more proof of your dicky-ness. A total turn-off."

Tyler looks shocked. "You're pissed at me because I insisted on walking you to Randolph? But I was going there myself."

"No, no, not that. I'm not insane."

"Then what?"

"You truly don't know?"

"You could waterboard my ass and I still wouldn't be able to tell you."

I continue walking again. "Newsflash, Tyler. Calling Dimitri 'nerd' like you're some meathead jock in an eighties teen flick was rude and dismissive. Not to mention totally *cliché.*"

Tyler chuckles.

"It's not funny. What are you going to do to poor Dimitri next? Stuff him into a locker? Dump a tray of food on him in the cafeteria and threaten to beat him up if he doesn't give you his lunch money?"

A look of extreme amusement has washed over Tyler's gorgeous but dicky face. "Wow," he says. "I'm such a dick."

"Glad you've seen the light."

"The biggest dick who ever lived."

"I realize you're mocking me," I say. "But the way you treated Dimitri was incredibly rude and immature. The simple truth is I've realized I need to *like* and *respect* a guy to continue feeling any kind of physical attraction to him beyond initial lust. And now that I've seen the way you treat people when you're frustrated or embarrassed, especially someone as nice as Dimitri, the animal attraction I initially felt for you the other night is long gone."

Tyler adjusts his backpack on his shoulder as we continue walking toward Randolph. "So let me get this straight. Despite our white-hot chemistry at the party a mere *two* days ago, and despite everything you overheard me saying to Dimitri about me changing my mind about that thing you asked me to do with you, you're now not the least bit attracted to me simply because I called the tutor guy 'nerd'?"

"The 'tutor guy' has a name. It's *Dimitri.* And no amount of muscles and swagger and sparkling blue eyes and perfect white teeth is going to make you attractive to me after witnessing you treating Dimitri like crap."

He laughs. "But, just to be clear, you *did* want to jump my bones *before* I opened my big mouth and treated Dimitri like crap?"

I don't reply.

"Come on. If you're going to reject me after I unwittingly poured my heart out to you back there, you should at least tell me the truth about that."

I shrug. "Okay, yes. I admit when you first jogged up to Dimitri, I thought my panties were going to burst into flames. But, now, sadly, I've peeked behind the curtain and found out you're the second coming of Emilio Estevez, and I'm totally and completely turned off."

Tyler bites his lip like he's trying not to laugh. "So, just to be really, *really* clear. If I hadn't screwed up and called Dimitri 'nerd' back there, you probably would have come to my place tonight to let me do that thing you're dying to do?"

I walk in silence.

"Come on, little freshman. You overheard me say all that stuff to Dimitri about you. The least you can do is give me that."

I twist my mouth, consider how honest I want to be, and decide I might as well tell the guy the whole truth. Why not? The truth hurts, after all. And Tyler Caldwell is one guy who deserves to feel a little pain. "Yes. To be honest, I was so insanely attracted to you when I saw you again today, even more so than at the party, that I probably would have come to your place tonight to let you pop my cherry. But, unfortunately, you had to go and open your big, stupid *Breakfast Clubby* mouth, and now my lady-boner for you has vanished into thin air. *Poof.*"

"*Poof?*"

"Poof."

"Huh." He stops walking and motions to a large brick building next to us. "This is Randolph."

I stop walking alongside him, adjust my backpack on my shoulder, and stare at him defiantly.

"Well, I must say, you've given me a lot to think about," Tyler says. "One thing you should know about me is I'm always striving to improve myself as a human being. Not just as a football player or athlete, but also as a man. So I appreciate you giving me something to meditate on. Oh, I meditate. Did I mention that? Helps me clear my rambling mind."

"Great. Glad to hear it. You're the freaking Dalai Lama. Maybe next time you meditate, you should think about being less of a dick to 'nerds.'"

"Yeah, that's definitely the take-away from this life lesson, for sure. 'Tyler Caldwell, you should be less of a dick to nerds.'" He looks at me wistfully. "Wow. I must admit I'm deeply disappointed your rampant sexual attraction to me...just... vanished. All because I called Dimitri 'nerd.'"

I shrug. "Sexual attraction, at least for me, is like a light switch, Tyler. On. Off. On." I look at him pointedly. "*Off.*"

"And I was so looking forward to giving you your first through fifth orgasms tonight, too."

My clit is suddenly tingling. "Oh, well. Sucks to be you."

"I guess so." He looks at his watch. "Oh, we'd better get to class." He motions politely toward the front entrance of Randolph. "After you, sweetheart."

"Thanks, sweetheart."

"Oh, hey, hold up one sec," Tyler says after I pass him.

"Just one quick thing."

I stop in the doorframe and turn around.

"I don't know if it makes any difference to your flaccid lady-boner or not, and I want you to know I fully respect your newfound flaccidity toward me either way. But I think maybe there's one small thing you should take into consideration before deciding once and for all I'm not the guy to make you see God for the first through fifth time tonight." He reaches into his pocket and pulls out his phone as he talks. "Do you happen to know that tutor guy's full name?"

"I believe I've mentioned the 'tutor guy' has a name. It's *Dimitri.*"

"But do you know his last name?"

My stomach tightens. Why do I suddenly feel like I'm walking into a trap here? "No."

Tyler swipes into his texts. "Yeah, I figured as much." He looks me dead in the eye, a devilish smirk curling one side of his mouth. "His name is Dimitri...*Nerdtowsky.*"

I close my eyes. *Shit.*

Tyler chuckles with glee. "And guess what Dimitri *Nerdtowsky's* self-proclaimed nickname is? Can you guess?"

I open my eyes to find Tyler holding his phone out to me, a smug look on his face.

"*Nerd,*" Tyler spits out, answering his own question. "Dimitri's nickname is *Nerd.* And if you don't believe me, then check out this text conversation between us in which I initially addressed him as 'Dimitri' and he signed off in his reply as 'Nerd.'"

I smash my lips together.

Tyler stuffs his phone into his front pocket, a grin on his face. "But, hey, thanks so much for chewing my ass. It was super fun." He chuckles. "Actually, as long as brutal honesty seems to be our *thing*, I should confess watching you get so hot and bothered about what a dick I was to poor Dimitri was highly... *arousing*." He laughs again and motions to the entrance to Randolph Hall. "After you, sweetheart. Make sure to save me a seat."

CHAPTER NINE

I march into Randolph Hall, my cheeks hot and my heart racing...and immediately spot a face in the crowd that brings a demonic smile to my face. The golden god himself, Jake Grayson, is sitting in a middle row of the lecture hall, surrounded by a bunch of athletic-looking dudes.

I turn to Tyler walking into the classroom behind me. "Oh, look, there's Jake," I say primly. "Hey, do you think the universe is trying to tell me something? You advised me to find a nice guy who'll buy me a cheeseburger before de-virginizing me and two days later, lo and behold, I find myself in a classroom with the one guy everyone in the world seems to think is the nicest, sweetest guy in the world."

"Fuck," Tyler mutters under his breath, his smug smile from a moment ago gone.

"I wonder if Jake likes cheeseburgers."

"Zooey, listen to me. Jake's not the guy for you."

But I'm not listening to him. I'm too busy holding my pinky to my mouth like Dr. Evil.

"Ty!" Jake shouts, as if on cue.

"Will you introduce us?" I ask, batting my eyelashes. "I heard he's super *nice*."

"Come on," Tyler says, grabbing my arm. But he doesn't

lead me toward Jake. He shoots a clipped wave toward Jake and the guys sitting with him and drags me toward two vacant seats in the front row.

I sit in the seat indicated by Tyler and pull out my laptop, my heart pounding in my ears. *Oh, my, this is going to be fun.*

Tyler leans in to my ear. "We both know you don't want Jake. If you wanted him over me, you would have flirted with him at the party when he was drooling all over you and asking everyone who you were."

"*What?*" I ask, floored.

"But you didn't," Tyler continues, obviously unaware he's just revealed something to me I didn't already know. "You went straight for *me*. And I went straight for you. Because we were magnet and steel. So fuck that bastard."

I don't reply. *Holy shit.*

A middle-aged woman with blonde, frizzy hair glides to a lectern at the front of the room and greets the class.

"To be continued, magnet," Tyler whispers, pulling away from me.

"We'll see about that, steel."

"Count on it."

The professor welcomes the class and, for the next twenty minutes, gives us an overview of Social Psychology and the structure of her ten-week class. "Your grade will be based on two things," the professor explains. "A final exam and a midterm project you'll complete with a partner." She explains that each partnership duo will devise and conduct a series of experiments to explore any social psychology theory and then submit a written analysis of their findings. "So let's go through the partner assignments, shall we?" the professor says, holding up a piece of paper. "And, please, nobody ask me to switch partners. Out there in the real world, you're going to have to work with colleagues or bosses you might not otherwise pick on occasion, so you might as well get used to doing that now."

I look at Tyler, my expression telling him he's the one person in this classroom I don't want as a partner. He holds up crossed fingers in reply, telling me he's praying to get assigned to me. In response, I flash him a look that says, *If I were assigned to you as my partner, I'd throw myself off a bridge.* And what does the cocky bastard do in reply to that? He winks and blows me a little kiss.

The professor reads off the first two names on her list and then makes small talk with the duo. After that, she repeats the exercise about eight more times before finally saying, "Tyler Caldwell?"

My stomach seizes. Please, God, don't let her say my name next. I don't have any desire to be attached at the hip to this egomaniac for the next five weeks, working on a project worth half my grade. Surely, if I were assigned to work with Tyler, we'd wind up having a one-night stand at some point, simply because he's gorgeous and sexy, and I'm only human. And then, following that, everything between us would feel tense and awkward, and our project would surely suffer. Not good.

Tyler raises his arm in response to the professor calling his name. "Hi, Professor."

The professor flashes Tyler a beaming smile. "Great game the other night. I lost my mind when you made that interception at the last minute. I thought I was going to pass out."

Tyler chuckles. "I had a similar reaction."

Everyone laughs.

"How on earth did you make that catch?" the professor asks, her eyes sparkling with obvious admiration. "It's like you had a jet pack on your back."

Tyler chuckles again. "It was equal parts adrenaline and luck."

"And *talent*," the professor adds. "Supernatural talent."

Tyler's teammates at the back of the room groan.

"Don't encourage him!" one of the guys sitting near Jake calls out.

"Oh, pipe down," the professor says playfully. "I'm just giving credit where it's due. That was one of the most acrobatic interceptions I've ever witnessed, and I've watched a lot of football in my life."

"Come on, Prof," one of the players in the back shouts. "Don't make his head even bigger than it already is. With all the interceptions Tyler's been racking up this season already, his head could barely fit through the doorway of the classroom as it is!"

Everyone laughs, including the professor and me.

"Okay, okay," the professor says gaily. She flashes a warm smile at Tyler. "Stay humble, Tyler. If not, you're going to get me into trouble here."

"Always."

The guys at the back of the room groan and scoff again.

The professor looks down at her paper again, smiling

from ear to ear. "Okay, Tyler. You want to know your partner assignment?"

Tyler looks at me and winks. "Make it a good one."

"Your partner is..."

My stomach squeezes. *Please, God, no.*

"*...Aaron Heckerling.*"

A loud cheer erupts from the guys at the back of the room. I turn toward the commotion just in time to see an attractive, dark-haired guy next to the golden god fist-pumping the air.

"Well, hello, Aaron," the professor says, chuckling at the guy's exuberance. "I take it you're familiar with Tyler here?"

"He's my boy," Aaron says. "My partner in crime."

"We live together," Tyler explains.

"Ah, well, in that case, I'll expect you two to turn in a particularly stellar project, seeing as how you'll be able to spend so much time working on it together."

"I've never seen that guy before in my life," Tyler deadpans, and everyone, including me, cracks up.

After reading off ten or so more pairings, the professor finally says my name.

"Here," I say, shooting my arm up. Oh, God, this is nerve-wracking. Give me a role with a script and I'm perfectly comfortable. Ask me to make small talk with a total stranger as myself, and I feel like I'm going to throw up.

The professor chats with me for a moment, eliciting the facts that I'm a freshman theater major and that I'm in this class to fulfill my science requirement. Finally, she says, "All right, Zooey. Your partner is ..."

I hold my breath.

"*Jake Grayson.*"

I laugh out loud, just as Tyler mutters, "Motherfucker."

I turn around and look at Jake several rows behind me. We exchange waves and polite smiles. And then I glance at Tyler and force down a giggle at the sight of him. He looks like he wants to punch a wall.

The professor fawns all over Jake for a while, telling him how magnificently he played the other night, and how much she admires his talent and skill, *and oh my God*, she hopes and prays we make it into another bowl game at the end of this season under his deft leadership! And all the while, Tyler's tense body language makes it clear he's losing his freaking mind. And, honestly, I'm not sad about it.

When the professor moves along to the next names on her list, I lean into Tyler's broad shoulder. "I have this weird feeling the universe is trying to tell me something. I'm just not sure what it is."

"It's telling you to be at my house at eight," he whispers back.

"Gee, I don't think so. I can't be sure but I think it's saying... Wait. Hang on." I put my hand to my ear like I'm listening to a faraway voice. "Oh. I think I hear it now. It's saying *Jaaaaaaaake.*"

The professor finishes reading from her partners list and wraps up the class. "Don't forget to exchange contact information with your partners, everyone. You're going to be working closely together for the next five weeks. Oh, and make sure you check the syllabus for the reading assignment. I'll see you on Wednesday!"

I lean into Tyler. "Best class *ever*."

"It's about to get a whole lot better," he mutters. With that, he lurches out of his seat and beelines up the aisle toward Jake and his teammates.

I watch Tyler striding up the steps. His movement is graceful and powerful. When he reaches Jake, he puts his muscled arm around his friend's shoulders like a mob boss, and whispers into his ear.

Dang it. If ever there was a time I could use some bionic hearing, now would be it. That handsome guy with dark hair who was paired with Tyler leans into the huddle. The three of them pow-wow. Jake fist-bumps Tyler and then the dark-haired guy, and the three of them head down the aisle toward me.

Immediately, I look down and begin packing up my laptop, awaiting Tyler's inevitable return. But when he still hasn't approached me in what seems like more than enough time, I look up. *Crap.* All three guys are talking to the professor at the lectern! *What the hell?* I watch the action closely, taking in the guys' facial expressions. Oh, man, those boys are all pouring on the charm. The professor's back is facing me, but her body language seems highly receptive to whatever they're saying. And now, all three boys appear to be saying variations of *"Thank you, Professor."* Suddenly, it's abundantly clear to me. I'm going to be partnered with Tyler Caldwell, whether I like it or not.

"Zooey Cartwright?" the professor calls out. She scans the crowd, apparently not remembering which student is me.

I walk toward the lectern like Anne Boleyn shuffling

stoically toward the chopping block.

"Hi, Zooey," the professor says warmly.

I glance at Tyler, and he smiles like an executioner unsheathing his sword.

"I don't know if you're aware that Jake here is the quarterback of the football team?" the professor says.

"Yes, of course." I glance at Jake and blush crimson when he flashes me a huge smile.

"Well, Jake was just telling me about some of the demands on his time, things he has to do each week that aren't necessarily required of anyone else on the team—or anyone else at the entire school, frankly. And so, because of Jake's special situation, he says he'd be extremely grateful if I'd make an exception to my 'no switching partners' rule, just this once."

My eyes flicker ever so briefly to Tyler, and he flashes me a look that's so cocky, I want to slap it off him.

"So, if it's okay with you," the professor continues, "I'm hoping you'll be amenable to a switch? Jake seems to think it would make the most sense for him and the team if he's paired with another player, preferably one on the offense, since those are the players who share Jake's practice schedule. Aaron here is a wide receiver so he'd be a good fit."

Oh, for the love of all things holy. What the hell kind of snow job is this? My dad played college ball, so I happen to know the offensive and defensive players attend the same practices at the same times. Yeah, Jake probably spends more time than other players watching films and working with his quarterback coach, but there's absolutely no reason why he and Aaron would have "the exact same practice schedule" any more than Jake and any defensive player. I look at the three guys. All of them are smiling at me. But Tyler's smile is nothing short of diabolical.

"Um. Sure. No problem," I say.

The professor looks at Tyler. "You're sure this swap will work for you, Tyler?"

"Yep. Anything to help Jake," Tyler replies.

The professor looks concerned. "You don't think you should maybe be assigned to a teammate, too, given the heavy demands on your time with practices and games and travel?"

I roll my eyes. What the heck happened to "Don't bother asking me to change partners"? Perhaps the professor more accurately should have said, "Don't bother asking me to change partners, *unless you're a handsome football star, in which case go right ahead.*"

"No, it's fine," Tyler says. "But thanks so much for asking. I've got a lot going on, for sure, but not quite as much as Jake. He's got to be ready to command the entire ship, as it were. I've just got to be ready to chase after whatever guy on the opposing team happens to be going after the little brown ball." He smiles like he's just uttered the understatement of the year, and the professor giggles.

Christ almighty. Of all the professors on this campus, I had to get the one who's a diehard football fan?

"If it helps Jake, then I'm more than happy to partner with Chloe here," Tyler adds magnanimously.

"*Zooey,*" the professor corrects.

One side of Tyler's mouth hitches up. "*Zooey.* So sorry."

"No problem, *Taylor,*" I say.

"*Tyler*," Tyler says. "Tyler Caldwell."

I return his smirk. "*Tyler*. So sorry."

The professor claps her hands together. "Okay, I'll see you all on Wednesday, then." She begins gathering her stuff, signaling this conversation is now over.

I sling my backpack over my shoulder and march toward the exit.

"Zooey!" the professor calls after me and I turn around, a fake smile on my face. "Be sure to get Tyler's contact information. You two will need to get together to map out your game plan for the next five weeks."

"Thanks for the reminder, Professor," Tyler says sweetly. "Yeah, we'll want to get together as soon as possible, for sure."

I nod. It's all I can muster at the moment. Without saying a word or even glancing at Tyler, I turn on my heel and march out of the classroom.

CHAPTER TEN

"No, I'm not 'elated' about it," I huff. Despite my best efforts to elude Tyler after Social Psych, he sprinted after me, and now he's tagging alongside me as I make my way toward my next class in North Campus. "I was honestly excited to partner with Jake."

Tyler scoffs. "Bah. I did you a huge favor, cupcake. Unless, of course, your goal in life is to never achieve orgasm as long as you live—in which case, yeah, I definitely thwarted that plan. Sorry, not sorry."

"Gee, that's not a preposterous leap in logic. Me being Jake's partner on a class project during my first year of college would lead to me *never* having a single orgasm throughout my *entire* life? How do you figure that one, *cupcake*?"

"I'm just connecting the dots," Tyler replies. "If I'd left you partnered with Jake for five weeks, you would have lost your virginity to him, no doubt about it." He rolls his eyes. "And that means you would have fallen in love with him, despite the fact that he's got the personality of paint drying, just because you're a newbie, and he looks the part of Mr. Right. Fast forward twenty years and ten babies later, and there you'd be, lying in bed one night after deeply unsatisfying sex with your boring-ass husband, and a little voice inside your head would whisper, I wonder if Tyler Caldwell would have been able to make me come the way my boring-ass husband never has?"

I scoff. "Careful, Tyler. Your jealousy is showing. Unless you've had sex with Jake yourself, you're in no position to comment on his sexual skills or lack thereof. Have you had sex with Jake?"

"Nope. I'm straight. But I've got intel straight from the horse's mouth." He lowers his voice. "What I'm about to tell you is highly confidential, okay? Seriously. You can't tell anyone."

"Fine."

He leans toward me. "For the last couple of years, Jake's been asking me for tips to use with his girlfriend. You know, *techniques.* Apparently, no matter what he tried with her, he just couldn't get her off. *Not once.* So, you see, all I'm trying to do here is protect you from a disastrous first time, followed by an entire lifetime of sexual dissatisfaction." He motions to the phrase on his shirt. "You're welcome."

"Thanks, but I don't want or need your protection," I say. "I'm quite confident I can find myself a guy who'll buy me a cheeseburger before de-virginizing me without your assistance."

We arrive at MacGowan Hall, the main building of the theater department, and I stop walking. "This is me," I say, motioning to the building. "Now fly and be free, Tyler Caldwell. I'll text you to figure out a time for us to work on our Social Psych project later this week, okay? Bye." I'm about to turn on my heel and walk into the building, but the devilish smile on Tyler's face stops me. "What?"

"Your next class is in MacGowan?"

A sinking feeling grips my stomach. "Yeah."

"Is it Modernizing Shakespeare by any chance?"

I close my eyes and exhale.

"Lucky you, I'm fulfilling my arts requirement with that class." He chuckles. "Gosh, when the universe works *this* hard to put two ridiculously good-looking people together, it'd be downright arrogant of them *not* to have sex, don't you think?"

"I'm not going to have sex with you, Tyler."

He smirks. "Oh, yes you are. You know it. I know it. The universe knows it. But we don't have time to discuss that right now—we've got to get to our Shakespeare class." He slides his hand into mine like he's been doing it for years, and my skin electrifies at his touch. "Come on, Zooey Cartwright. If we're late, we might not be able to find two seats together."

CHAPTER ELEVEN

Fate. It's a fickle little bitch.

This morning as I headed off to my first day of classes around nine, I never wanted to see Tyler Caldwell again. I told myself if I happened to see him on campus, I'd bolt in the opposite direction. And now it's six o'clock on the same day, and I'm walking to Tyler's house to brainstorm not one but *two* partner projects with him. That's right. I've been assigned as Tyler's partner for *two* class projects thanks to my Shakespeare professor's decision to assign partners based on last names.

I turn off the sidewalk and onto the front walkway of Tyler's house, my mind reeling. Of course, now that I'll be working closely with Tyler on *two* projects, it's especially clear to me I simply *cannot* sleep with him. Not when my grade in two classes depends on me being able to work with him for five long weeks. I suppose once both our projects are turned in, we *might* get together for one night of meaningless sex, assuming I don't hate his guts by then. But for now, considering the situation, I'm absolutely determined that no sex shall transpire between Tyler Caldwell and me.

I reach Tyler's front door, take a deep breath, and knock. A moment later, there he is. Standing in the doorframe. Freshly showered. Smelling of soap. He's holding a barbeque spatula and wearing an apron that reads Kiss the Cook! And the look on Tyler's face? He looks like a spider welcoming a fly into his web.

"You're early, partner," Tyler says. "Well, aren't you an eager little beaver."

"I'm not eager, just prompt," I say stiffly, marching through the door. "Now that we're double-stuck together, we've got a ridiculous amount of work to do."

"*Double-stuck?* Oh, baby. I love it when you talk dirty to me."

I stride into the living room, feeling like a dork for lobbing such a softball to him...even though, honestly, I don't understand how "double-stuck" could possibly be any kind of sexual innuendo. I stop short. The song blaring through the overhead speakers is "Let's Get It On" by Marvin Gaye. I whirl around to face Tyler. "No, Tyler."

Tyler smiles. "What?"

I point up, referencing the song.

"*Oh.* You think I'm sending you some sort of coded message with this song? No, cupcake. This is a random playlist. Pure coincidence. But if it makes you feel better, I'll skip ahead to the next song." He pulls out his phone and presses a button, and a new song begins. "I'll Make Love to You" by Boyz II Men. "Is that better, sweetheart?"

I stare at him, determined not to smile, but when he starts singing along to the cheesy lyrics, I can't help myself.

"I'm wearing you down," Tyler says.

"I'm only smiling because you're singing off-key," I say. "My smile means only that I find you amusing. Nothing more."

"Okay. I respect that. I'll change the song, then. Enough playing around. Sorry. It was worth a try." He presses a button on his phone, and "I Want Your Sex" by George Michael begins blaring.

I giggle.

"I could do this forever, babe," he says. He winks.

"Oh, I'm sure you could."

"You want another one?" he asks.

"No, leave it here. I like George."

"So do I. 'Careless Whisper' is one of my all-time favorites. When I sing you that one, you're going to drop your panties for me on the spot."

I bite my lip. I'm not sure Tyler is going to need to sing "Careless Whisper" to get me to do that. Indeed, the sexy look he's shooting me at the moment would surely make a nun rip off her habit.

"Oh, on a totally unrelated topic," Tyler says. "I hope you don't mind I asked my roommates to make themselves scarce tonight. I figured a girl like you would want to talk about social psychology and Shakespeare without any of them around."

My clit pulses. "A girl like me?"

"*A freshman*." Another smile. "I hope you're hungry, little freshman." He motions to a nearby table laid out with two plates of food. "Because I made us cheeseburgers."

CHAPTER TWELVE

For the past forty-five minutes or so, Tyler and I have been sitting at his table, eating our cheeseburgers and salad, and chatting about surprisingly nonsexual things. True, the songs playing during our meal have been about sex, sex, and more sex—either doing it or desperately wanting to do it. And, yes, Tyler has stopped midsentence on several occasions to suddenly and enthusiastically sing along with some particularly cheesy lyrics. His enthusiastic but off-key rendition of the chorus of "Pour Some Sugar on Me" was a highlight, I must admit. But, mostly, we've just...talked. And I've loved every minute of it.

Tyler puts down his napkin onto his empty plate and leans back in his chair. "You want to brainstorm our Shakespeare project now, partner?"

Wow, I'm shocked. I thought it'd be like wrangling cats to get Tyler to work on our Shakespeare project tonight. "That'd be awesome," I say. "We've got a lot to do."

It's an understatement. Our Modernizing Shakespeare assignment is a doozy. We're required to select any scene from Shakespeare, write a five-page paper dissecting its themes and language, and then write a contemporary scene inspired by it. And then, after all that, we've still got to do the biggest task of all. Perform *both* scenes—the original Shakespearean one and the contemporary scene we've created—in front of our entire class.

After a bit of back and forth, Tyler and I settle on our Shakespearean scene: when Romeo meets Juliet for the first time at a masquerade ball.

"So, this scene is about Romeo trying to get into Juliet's pants?" Tyler asks.

"Yup. We shouldn't have any trouble writing a contemporary scene inspired by this one, huh?"

Tyler laughs. "Art imitating life, definitely." He gets up from his seat. "We threw a Mardi Gras-themed party at the house last year. I'm pretty sure we've got some leftover masks. Hang on." He leaves and returns a moment later, holding two sparkling masks. "Do these look like sixteenth century masquerade masks?"

"They're perfect." I take one of the masks from Tyler and slip it on.

"Wow, that's sexy," he says, putting on the other mask. "No wonder Romeo wanted to get into Juliet's pants. *Damn, girl.*"

I giggle. "Just read the scene, Romeo."

We read through the scene in our masks, right up to the spot where the stage direction tells us Romeo kisses Juliet.

"This is where we'll kiss," I say tightly.

"Great. Let's kiss."

"Not tonight," I say, my cheeks coloring. "Let's just read through the scene tonight and figure out our blocking another night."

"Blocking?"

"Our movements."

"But we're going to kiss for real when we perform it, right?"

"Of course."

"So, we should practice kissing now. There are a thousand ways to kiss, after all. We need to make sure we kiss the way Romeo and Juliet would have done it."

I swallow hard. If I kiss this boy tonight, even as chastely as Romeo and Juliet would have kissed at their first meeting, I'm positive I'll lose all my willpower and agree to sleep with him. "Not tonight," I insist. "We'll practice the kiss another time. Say your next line."

Tyler exhales and begrudgingly continues the scene. But, quickly, it's time for Romeo and Juliet's second kiss of the scene.

"And here we'll kiss again," I say flatly.

Tyler looks up from his book. "This is stupid. We should practice kissing now. Practice makes perfect, after all."

"Not tonight."

Tyler pulls off his mask and tosses it onto the table. I follow suit.

"You seem stressed, little freshman," he says. "Let's go sit on the couch and talk this over." Without waiting for my reply, he pulls me up from my chair and leads me to the couch.

"Okay, so are you ready to talk about our Social Psych project now?" I ask weakly, settling myself on the far end of the couch from Tyler.

"No," he replies. "I was thinking we'd relax for a bit and then rehearse those two kisses."

"I don't think I'll be able to 'relax for a bit' until we've figured out our topic for our Social Psych project. I'm stressed about it, to be honest."

Tyler smiles. "All right. Social Psych it is. I definitely want you nice and relaxed for me tonight."

I abruptly grab a notepad off the coffee table. "Great. Let's brainstorm topics for our experiments."

Shockingly, Tyler doesn't argue with me. Instead, he launches into an earnest discussion about the project—and, twenty minutes later, we've already got a list of twelve potential topics for experiments.

"Okay," I say, looking down at our list. "If you had to choose our general topic right now, which one would it be?"

"The power of persuasion," Tyler says without hesitation.

"Any specific aspect?"

"Yes, thank you for asking. I'm curious to know what would persuade a beautiful, curly-headed freshman theater major at UCLA to want to have sex with an extremely well-endowed free safety named Tyler Caldwell."

I bite my lip. "Interesting query. Unfortunately, I think that's a bit specific for a social psych experiment. Kind of niche-y, I'd say."

"You think?"

"I do. Although there might be some cross-over with my preferred topic."

"Which is?"

"I'd like to explore the halo effect."

"What's that, again?"

Damn. This is exactly what I was worried about when I got stuck with a football player as a partner. That I'd be forced to work with a jock who doesn't give a crap about his school work, and I'd have to do all the work for both of us.

I lean back into the sofa, my body language tight. "It was in the reading assignment, Tyler."

He smiles. "I haven't done the reading assignment yet."

I flash him an annoyed look that says, *Yeah, no shit.*

Tyler's smile vanishes. He flips his pen onto the coffee table. "Okay, let me explain something to you, Zooey Cartwright. In all seriousness." He sighs. "Playing football at a school like UCLA, especially on scholarship, is a *huge* fucking deal. It's a full-time job on top of all my classes. Every day except Sundays, I've got massive time commitments on top of my classes and homework. Take today, for instance. I was at the gym before five this morning. Worked out for close to three hours. After that, I went to two classes, after which I stuffed some food into my mouth, and then high-tailed it to a three-hour practice that kicked my ass. Right after that, I had a cryogenics session with a trainer that I skipped out early on so I could swing by the store to buy ingredients for the awesome dinner I planned to make for a pretty theater major who was coming over to my house later that evening. And then I raced home with just enough time to shower, grill up gourmet cheeseburgers, and create a playlist of bonin' songs intended to subliminally persuade said pretty theater major to have sex with me tonight." He flashes me a charming smile. "Now when the hell was I supposed to do the Social Psych reading on top of all that? It's still the first day of school, dude. You think *maybe* your expectations for me are a bit unrealistic?"

My cheeks bloom. "I'm sorry. I didn't...realize."

"I'll pull my weight in this partnership. That's a promise. You just need to be patient with me if I need to play catch-up sometimes. I typically do my reading on Sundays. That's my only free day of the week."

"I get it. I'm sorry. I didn't mean to sound so pissy. Forgive me."

"It's okay."

I shift in my seat, feeling stupid. "So, um..." I clear my throat. "The halo effect. It's when people think good-looking people are smarter and cooler and funnier than everyone else, even when in reality they might be stupid or boring. Add athleticism or any kind of celebrity status into the mix, and the halo effect supposedly goes through the roof."

"You think the halo effect is real?"

"I know it is. Just look at my reaction to you. I wanted to sleep with you based on looks alone, before I'd even spoken two words to you. You could have been the stupidest, most boring guy in the world, and I didn't care simply because you're gorgeous. Halo effect."

"Sounds like basic animal attraction to me. I wanted to have sex with you the second I saw you, too, even before I found out you're a total weirdo." He grins. "Was that the halo effect, too?"

I open my mouth and close it. "I'm not sure. Maybe?"

"At least from my experience," Tyler continues, "the halo effect is a wash. For all the times someone thinks great things about me based on my looks or athleticism alone, someone else assumes bad stuff about me."

"Like what?"

He grins wickedly. "That I'm the kind of guy who runs around calling other guys 'nerd.'"

I shoot him a snarky look.

"Seriously, though, people tend to think I'm a dumb jock or a complete douchebag. Or that I'm some kind of raging manwhore who can't keep his dick in his pants. I'm constantly having to disprove people's stereotypical, preconceived notions about me."

"Yeah, well, I've got to stop you right there, cupcake. If you don't want people assuming you're a meathead manwhore who can't keep his dick in his pants, then how about you stop wearing shirts that say God's Gift to Womankind and You're Welcome!"

Tyler holds up his finger. "Ah. The shirts prove my point. Is it possible you're holding my T-shirts against me *because* of my looks? Imagine if Dimitri wore one of my message shirts. You wouldn't think he's a douchebag manwhore for a split second. You'd think he's funny and charming. You'd probably think he was being sarcastic and, therefore, that he's self-deprecating and humble."

I make a face like he's got a point.

"So it's your *assumptions* about me, based on my looks, that turn me into a perceived egomaniac when I wear them. As a point of fact, there's a very good reason I wear those shirts."

"You mean besides the shirts implicitly warning Stage Five Clingers to stay the hell away?"

"Yeah, that was an incidental benefit I discovered after the fact. The reason I *started* wearing those shirts was because I realized I could make them the foundation of my brand."

"Your *brand*?"

Tyler's face lights up. "Think about it. Which NFL players do you think get the biggest commercials and merchandizing deals? The best players on the field?" He shakes his head. "Talent's only one part of the equation. The thing that makes a guy the most marketable off the field is a huge personality. He's got to be instantly recognizable. A guy everyone loves or loves to hate. So I'm creating my brand now to lay the foundation for the global empire I'll be building when I'm in the NFL."

"Your *empire*?"

"Mark my words, I'll be a household name during my rookie season. And by the end of my career, my impact's going to reach far beyond football. One day, I'll be like Muhammad Ali. Michael Jordan. Michael Phelps. A global *brand*."

"And all because you wear message tees?"

"No. Of course, not. Message tees will be the initial hook that's going to make me stand out at first. They'll be my gateway into a full sportswear line. Shoes. Nike commercials. And all that will give me the seed money for what I want to do when my playing days are over—invest in real estate." He taps his temple. "I'm a business major, baby. I know exactly what I'm doing. And it all starts with the message T-shirts. Just watch."

I'm blown away. "How did you start wearing the T-shirts in the first place?"

"By chance. One day during my senior year in high school, I wore a T-shirt that said Heartbreaker. I think I got it at American Apparel or wherever, just because I thought it was funny. But then, after I'd worn it a couple of times, some girls on the pep squad wore 'Heartbreaker' shirts the day of a big game to show support for me. So that gave me an idea. I gathered all my savings and bought a bunch of blank T-shirts and had 'Heartbreaker' silkscreened onto them. And then I sold them, with a dollar from each sale going to charity. *Boom.* They sold out instantly. So I reinvested my profits and bought more shirts. Thought up some new phrases. Wore the new phrases to make them seem cool. Put the shirts on sale with a buck from each sale going to charity. *Boom.* Sold out of those in lightning speed, too. And on and on. I was unstoppable. As long as I wore the new message first for a bit, then the world wanted it. Everyone wanted to dress like Tyler Caldwell. By the time I graduated, I had a drawer full of different message T-shirts, a nice chunk of change for my charity, and enough cash to buy myself a motorcycle for college."

My jaw is hanging open. "And you seriously question if the halo effect is real? Tyler, if anyone else had worn those shirts, nobody would have cared. I mean, jeez, look what happened today in Social Psych. The professor said don't ask to switch partners, and then three handsome football players asked to switch partners, and she couldn't switch for you guys fast enough. Just imagine if Dimitri had asked her to change partners. Or if he'd worn those message shirts in high school. You think anyone would have bought those shirts from him?"

Tyler's eyes light up. "That's it! That's our experiment. We'll test out the halo effect. It'll be me versus Dimitri. Let's see if you're right about that."

I squeal. "I *love* it. You think Dimitri will help us out?"

"Oh, I'm sure he will. But if you ask your roommate to help us, too, he'll be Johnny on the Spot, for sure."

"Perfect."

Tyler puts his notepad on the coffee table and pointedly scoots closer to me on the couch. "So is that enough work for our first night, taskmaster?"

"Yeah, I think we got a ton accomplished tonight. Don't you?"

"I do." He scoots even closer to me, his eyes darkening with heat. "So are you feeling relaxed now, little freshman?"

My crotch flutters. "Um. Right this very second? No. Actually."

"*No?*" He smiles. "Why not?"

"Because you're sitting two inches away from me, looking at me like you want to swallow me whole."

Tyler's smile widens, but he doesn't argue the point.

I exhale. "Tyler, we're not going to have sex tonight. We can't."

"Why not?"

"Because we're going to be working closely together for the next five weeks and seeing each other in class for five more weeks after that. Plus, now that I've gotten to know you a bit, and I actually kind of don't hate you, I'm positive a one-night stand with you would be hard for me to handle. If I'm being perfectly honest, I'd probably want to have sex with you again after that first time. And I wouldn't know how to act around you in our classes after our one-night stand. I'd worry every time I sat down within four rows of you, you'd be like, 'Stalker! Stage Five Clinger! Don't slash my tires!' and I'd be like, 'Dude, chill. I'm enrolled in this class, remember?'"

Tyler chuckles and snakes one arm around my shoulders.

"Why do you assume we'd have nothing but a one-night stand?"

I look at him like he's on crack. "Because that's what you explicitly said is the only item on the Tyler Caldwell menu. One night and nothing more, remember?"

Tyler's eyes are locked on mine. He's so close, I feel his body heat. He rests his free hand on my thigh. "I said that because you were a hot girl at a party who wanted to have sex with a guy wearing a douchey message T-shirt. But now you're Zooey Cartwright, the pretty, smart, funny weirdo-theater-major I'm going to be hanging out with for the next five weeks. Under the circumstances, I think the intelligent thing for me to do would be to adapt and change the Tyler Caldwell menu." He grins. "'Intelligence is the ability to adapt to change.' Stephen Hawking."

"What are you suggesting?"

"I'm suggesting we have sex every time we get together to work on our projects over the next five weeks. Beginning tonight."

My lips part.

"Now, just to be clear," he adds. "I'll only be able to see you Monday through Wednesday for the next five weeks. That's all I can manage with my schedule. But when I see you, hell yeah, I'm suggesting we have lots and lots of awesome sex."

My mind is racing. I can't breathe.

"Think of it like a third partner project," he says softly, leaning close to my face. "We'll call it 'The Miseducation of Zooey Cartwright.' For five weeks, Monday through Wednesday, I'll teach you everything you need to know about sex. And when you graduate from my five-week course, you'll be ready to bone with the best of 'em, baby."

My heart is exploding with excitement. I don't want to look a gift horse in the mouth by asking too many questions—because, God knows, what Tyler's offering me is a thousand times more enticing to me than any of my cherry-popping one-night-stand fantasies. But I can't go into this with any misunderstandings. "And what happens when the five weeks are over?" I ask. "After we turn in our midterm projects, we'll still have two classes together, twice a week, for another five weeks. Won't that be awkward?"

"Not if we agree up front that our miseducation project will last five weeks and nothing more. To be honest, I fully expect you to be chomping at the bit to try out all your newly acquired sex-kitten skills on some other dudes by the time we get to the five-week mark."

"Oh, so you're assuming I wouldn't have sex with anyone else during the five weeks of my 'miseducation'?"

Tyler's eyes burst into flames. "That's nonnegotiable. You'll be my very own little hunk of clay to mold. All mine. It's gonna be a huge turn-on for me to know I'm your first for anything and everything we do, and I don't want anyone else fucking that up for me. But after the five weeks are up, knock yourself out, baby."

My heart is thudding noisily in my ears. "I'd want the same promise from you," I say. "I'd want you to have sex with only me during the entire five weeks."

"There's no logical reason for that arrangement. You're not my first. I'm not your hunk of clay to mold."

"Yeah, well, I don't want to wonder where else your 'hunk

of clay' has been during the five weeks you're sticking it inside me."

Tyler chuckles. "Fair enough. Okay, deal. Any other conditions?"

I feel dizzy. I shake my head.

"Great. But, remember, at the end of five weeks, we're friends. If you see me talking to someone else in class or at the book store, you've got to promise you won't slash my tires or light up my phone with fifty batshit crazy texts in an hour. *Friends.*"

"I understand." My face feels hot. My skin is sizzling. I can't believe this is happening. "So what happens now?" I whisper.

"This." He licks his lips, leans forward, and kisses me—and, instantly, my body explodes with arousal. I slide my arms around his neck and return his kiss passionately. In response, he pulls me toward him greedily, guiding me to sit on his lap, and I straddle him while continuing to kiss him. He cups my face in his palms and absolutely devours me while I rub my crotch furiously against his bulge.

Still kissing me, Tyler stands, taking me with him, and strides with me in his strong arms toward the staircase.

"You don't want to work on Shakespeare a bit more?" I whisper into his lips. But, of course, I'm joking.

"Shakespeare can go fuck himself," Tyler grits out. "That fucker is dead. I'm alive and hard as a rock, and I've never wanted a girl as much as I want you, Zooey Cartwright."

CHAPTER THIRTEEN

For the past twenty minutes, Tyler and I have been lying on his bed, both of us fully clothed, kissing and touching and groping and gyrating against each other. At this point, I'm so turned on, I feel like I'm about to explode. I don't know if Tyler's a mad genius or what, but this tactic of making out with me fully clothed for so long is making me ache so much, I want to grab him by his ears and scream, "Let's get naked already, for the love of God!"

As we continue kissing and groping each other, my fingers migrate to that delectable hard bulge behind his jeans. Oh, man, I'm dying to see it naked and in all its glory. I squeeze his hardness, and he groans into our kiss.

"You're so sexy," he whispers into my mouth. "You turn me on so much."

Then let's get naked.

"You want to get naked?" he whispers, reading my mind.

Hallelujah! "Mmm hmm," I say, excitement flooding me.

"Is that a yes?" he whispers. "I need an actual 'yes.'"

"Yes," I whisper. I'm trembling.

Tyler takes a deep breath. "Every step of the way, I'll need to hear a yes from you. If you say 'no' at any time, I'll stop whatever I'm doing."

I breathe a huge sigh of relief. Until this very moment, I didn't realize I was feeling anxiety about what we're about to do. "Thank you."

Tyler takes a deep, shaky breath, like he's trying to manage extreme physical pain. "So you wanna get naked, then?"

My heart is pounding. "*Yes.*"

Without further ado, he sits up and slowly peels off his shirt, baring his muscled torso to me for the first time, and my eyes pop out of my head.

"Yes!" I blurt.

He chuckles and peels off his jeans, revealing gray boxer briefs covering the clear outline of a hard shaft and tip. *Oh, dear God.* My clit has never ached like this before. My entire body feels on the verge of a total and complete meltdown. I hold my breath, waiting for Tyler to peel off his briefs, but he doesn't. Instead, he reaches to pull off my shirt.

"What about your underwear?" I ask as my shirt slips past my face. "Aren't you going to take those off?"

"Patience, eager beaver." He reaches behind my back and deftly unlatches my bra. And that's that. I'm now sitting before him, my breasts bared to him. It's the first time I've shown my naked torso to a guy in my life. My instinct is to cross my arms, but I somehow refrain.

"Have you ever been naked with a guy before?" Tyler asks softly. He looks incredibly aroused.

My nipples are tingling. I look down at myself. They're two hard, little pebbles. "This is the first time."

Tyler's eyes are on fire. "They're perfect." He looks from my chest to my face. "You're perfect, Zooey."

I swallow hard. "Well, it's not like I can take any credit for my boobs. This is how they sprouted, whether I wanted them to or not. They just grew and grew, and I kept thinking, Hey—"

"*Zooey.*"

I shut my mouth.

"Are you nervous, sweetheart?"

I press my lips together and nod. I'm shaking.

"Nervous like you want to slow down?"

I shake my head. "Nervous like I can't wait to go, go, go."

He laughs. "Excellent. Lie back, baby. You don't need to do a thing. Just relax and I'll handle everything."

I lie back, still trembling, and Tyler pulls off my shorts, leaving us both in our underwear, and then he leans down and begins caressing and kissing and licking my breasts and nipples. As he kisses me, one of Tyler's hands migrates toward the waistband of my underwear. A whimper of excitement escapes my mouth.

Instantly, Tyler's face snaps up from my breasts, like he's double-checking I'm still good.

"*Yes,*" I whisper, running my fingers through his hair. "Yes, yes, yes."

Tyler smiles, lowers his head, and devours my left nipple just as he slips his fingertips inside the waistband of my undies. I make a cooing sound I've never made before as his fingers find my wetness and gently stroke my tip.

Oh, crap. Oh, jeez. Holy hell. His fingers are doing magical things to me. I mean, oh my God—really, really magical things! I grip his bicep. Dig my nails into his flesh. Grip the sheet underneath me. Arch my back feverishly, shoving my pelvis into his touch. *Oh, hot damn, that feels good. Oh, motherfuck.* I coo again. And then begin gyrating like a stripper on a pole, my body craving something it's never tasted before but inherently knows it wants.

Tyler tugs on my panties, dragging them over my hips, so I help him out and get those suckers off like they're on fire. And now I'm naked on the bed, laid out for him like a picnic lunch. And I don't know if it was all that making out we did at first, but I've never been so wet in my life. *I'm ready.*

"I'm going to take off my briefs now," he whispers hoarsely.

I'm shivering with excitement. I open my mouth, and that little whimper comes out again.

"Yes?" he whispers.

I nod like a bobble-head doll. "*Yes.*"

He stands at the side of the bed and pulls down his briefs, and my jaw drops when his hard-on springs to freedom.

"Holy crap."

Tyler grins. "You ever seen one before?"

"Not in person. Is that entire thing really supposed to fit inside me?"

"It'll fit like a glove." He crawls onto the bed next to me, his massive erection straining toward his ripped abs, and a moment later, I feel the delicious dual sensations of his warm skin pressing against mine and his hard dick poking me in the thigh.

"Your body is designed for mine," he whispers. He rubs his tip against my thigh and moans. "You'll see. We're going to be a perfect fit." He lets out a shaky exhale. "There's no rush, though. There's plenty we can do without me putting it in. It doesn't have to happen tonight."

"No, tonight's the night," I whisper urgently. "As soon as possible."

He chuckles. "Patience, eager beaver." He slides his hand between my legs again. His fingers dip inside me and begin moving in and out of me in languid, gentle strokes. After a while, he begins trailing kisses down my belly as he continues to massage me. Down, down, down his hungry mouth goes toward his moving fingers. But just before his lips reach their final destination, I reflexively clamp my thighs shut.

Tyler doesn't miss a beat. He gently pushes my legs apart while continuing to kiss and lick the flesh right above my sex. "I can't wait to taste you," he says softly. "It's gonna get me off."

I take a deep breath and open my legs again—and two seconds later, Tyler's warm, wet tongue lands on my clit and begins lapping at me energetically. I let out a little yelp, shocked at how good it feels. "Oh Mylanta, that's nice."

Tyler chuckles into my crotch, and his warm breath tickles my most sensitive flesh. His fingers begin moving in and out of me again as he eats me, sending every molecule in my body vibrating, all at once.

In short order, I'm shuddering with pleasure. Panting. Gasping for air. Groaning. I grip the sheet. Spit out a long string of expletives. Followed by an incredibly embarrassing, guttural moan. I throw my head back. "This feels so good," I grit out. "Oh, Tyler."

Tyler shifts position and hunkers down between my legs like he's planning to stay a while. He gently pushes my legs open even wider—opening my folds to him like a blooming rose—

and, damn it, I reflexively clamp my legs again, squeezing the poor guy's head like a walnut in a nutcracker.

But Tyler's not fazed. He looks up from his meal while he slowly pushes my thighs apart. "Yes?"

I take a deep breath and speak on my exhale. "*Yes.*"

"Clear your mind, baby. There's no shame here. You taste amazing. I'm absolutely loving this. Just enjoy it."

I concentrate on clearing my mind as he continues his delicious work—and soon, I'll be damned, I feel something brewing inside me I've never felt before. A long, low moan escapes me. The muscles at my epicenter flutter. Tighten. My clit is tingling and swollen. It kind of hurts, actually. But it's a pain that feels oh-so good. A wave of pleasure rises sharply inside me. A tsunami looms and threatens to consume me. I feel it hovering over me in suspended animation, waiting to crash down.

"Oh, shit," I grit out, gripping the bedsheet with white knuckles underneath me. "I think... Oh, Jesus."

Tyler doubles down on what he's doing. He's doing magical things to me with his tongue and fingers.

"Tyler," I whisper. "Oh, God. I'm about to come, I think."

A deep-seated coiling overtakes my deepest muscles. I'm a rubber band about to snap. I look down and see Tyler's beautiful, bobbing head between my legs. His muscled shoulders. The tattoos on his bulging arms. I listen to the lapping sounds his tongue and lips are making as he eats me. The sounds of his breathing. His occasional growls. I peek at his hard dick. Its tip is wet and shiny. I imagine myself licking it like a lollipop. *And that does it.* Heat flashes into my clit almost painfully. Every muscle in my body tightens, all at once. My skin pricks with goose bumps. My toes curl. And then...

Oh, God. Jesus, Mary, and Joseph. Yes! "Oh!" I shout. "Oh, my God! I'm...*ooooh, Tyler!*"

My muscles surrounding Tyler's fingers begin squeezing and clenching in rhythmic waves, shooting spasms of pleasure throughout my core. It's a sensation of pure bliss like nothing I've felt before. Heaven. Unmitigated ecstasy. *Rapture.*

All of a sudden, Tyler's at my mouth, smiling and laughing. Cooing about how sexy I am. Kissing me.

"I came," I whisper after the waves of pleasure have subsided. I cup his cheeks with my palms. "You did it!"

"*You* did it."

"I did it!" I pull him toward me and kiss him, my heart bursting. This moment is perfect. I can't imagine doing this with anyone but Tyler, exactly like this. How could I have been so stupid as to think I could give my virginity away to some random dude at a party? And without even bothering to mention it was my first time? I was a fool.

Our kiss is ramping up. I grab Tyler's hard dick, eager to give him pleasure the way he's done for me. But he breaks away from our kiss, panting, and touches my hand. "Like this, sweetheart." He repositions my hand and shows me how to move it. "Yeah, that's nice. A little more pressure. Oh yeah, that's really nice."

"Show me," I say.

"You're doing it."

"No, show me how you do it to yourself."

Tyler rolls onto his side next to me and jerks himself off

while I study the movement of his hand. After a moment, I take over the job for him.

"Like this?"

"Yup," he says, his voice tight. "*Exactly.*" His dick feels silky smooth in my hand. It's turning me on to stroke him. But after not too long, Tyler inhales sharply and puts his hand on mine, stopping my movement. "I'm about to lose it," he explains, his voice taut. "If you want to give a guy your first hand job to completion, then keep going. If you want me to be able to put it inside you in the very near future, then you've got to stop."

I release him from my grip, serenity flooding me. I know exactly what I want. And it isn't to give Tyler Caldwell my first hand job. *I want this boy inside me, pronto.* "Put on a condom," I whisper, my eyes blazing. I lie down and arch my back, jutting my breasts and peaked nipples into the air toward him. "I want you inside me, Tyler. *I'm ready.*"

CHAPTER FOURTEEN

"Kinda looks like a kielbasa wearing rain slicker," I say and instantly regret it. *Come on, Zooey! Now's not the time for jokes!*

"A little advice?" Tyler says. "There's never a good time to make fun of a guy's dick. But especially not when he's about to stick it inside you."

"Sorry. I guess I'm a little more nervous than I realized."

Tyler touches my hair. "It's gonna be great. Well, as great as it can be your first time. From what I've been told, the first time for girls is often even more of a mind-fuck than a body-fuck."

"Was it a mind-fuck for you?"

"No. Just a body-fuck. A blink-and-it's-over body-fuck."

"Was your first time with another virgin?"

He snorts. "No." He leaves it at that.

"Then how do you know the first time is a mind-fuck for girls? Do you ask girls to fill out an exit survey every time you de-virginize them?"

"You're my first virgin. I know about the first time being a mind-fuck because my sister told me."

I grimace. "Now that's a close sibling relationship."

Tyler shrugs. "She just wanted to make sure, if ever I found myself in the present situation, I'd do a great job for the girl. Apparently, my sister's experience was highly disappointing."

"Well, tell your sister thanks from me."

"I won't tell my sister a damned thing. Tell whoever you want about this, but Tyler Caldwell doesn't de-virginize and tell." He winks.

Okay, seriously now. Is this guy for real? I poke his muscular arm to confirm he's not a figment of my imagination. How the heck did a douchebag at a party turn out to be Prince Charming? "Thank you for taking such good care of me," I whisper. "I appreciate it."

"I'm pretty sure it's me who should be thanking you, sweetheart. This is so fucking hot for me. Believe me, I'm loving it." He takes a deep breath. "Okay, so let's get some music going, eager beaver. I made the perfect de-virginization playlist for you."

"I heard it downstairs, remember?"

Tyler swats at the air. "That playlist was meant to be a joke. Sort of. This is serious now. This moment is going to be a lifelong memory for you. Ten years from now you'll be swapping stories with your friends about how each of you lost your V cards. And when you tell your story, I want your friends to say, 'Damn, that guy picked the perfect song.'"

"Yeah, and then I'll reply nonchalantly, Oh, did I mention the guy who took my virginity was the world-famous football player, Tyler Caldwell of the...?"

"Cowboys."

"He's the league leader in tackles and interceptions and defensive touchdowns."

Tyler flashes me an adorable smile. "And sacks and forced fumbles."

"Oh, yes, of course."

We share a smile.

God, he's gorgeous.

"Cue the song, Tyler," I whisper. "I'm ready."

Tyler rolls over to his nightstand and grabs his phone, and a song I don't know begins playing. "'Crash into Me' by Dave Matthews Band," Tyler says, answering my unspoken question. "I decided this one will never go out of style. You'll never look back and be bummed this song was the soundtrack for this particular memory."

My heart swells. "Thank you."

"So, let's get you ramped up and begging for it, shall we?"

"*Yes.*"

He hunkers down between my legs...and I'll be damned, after only a few minutes of him licking me again, I have the second orgasm of my life. And it's even better than the first one.

When my body finishes warping from the inside out, Tyler slithers up to my face, licking his lips. His eyes are blazing. He opens his mouth to speak.

"Yes," I blurt, cutting him off before he's said a word.

He smiles, crawls on top of me, presses his warm, hulking body onto mine, places his fingers inside me briefly, like he's finding his target, and then slowly, ever so slowly...*oh my God*... he's inside me. *He's inside me!* As deep as a man can possibly go! He's splitting me in two! Impaling me! And it doesn't even hurt!

"That's just the tip," he whispers.

Oh.

"Yes?" he grits out.

"*Yes.*"

I've no sooner said the magic word than a jolt of pain flashes through me, making me gasp.

Tyler freezes on top of me.

"Is that all the way?" I gasp.

"Half-way."

Oh, crap, there's more? I take a deep breath. "Keep going."

He pushes in slowly. "That's all the way." He lets out a shaky breath. "Oh, Jesus, Zooey, you feel so fucking good."

"I do?"

"Oh, God. So good." He takes a deep breath. "I'm gonna move inside you now. In and out. I'll kiss you while I do it. Oh, Jesus. This feels good." He lets out a shaky breath. "Yes?"

I nod.

"*Yes?*" he grits out. He sounds like a man hanging on the edge of a cliff by his fingernails.

"Yes."

Tyler moves slowly in and out of me. He's kissing me gently, touching my face, my hair, whispering into my ear that I feel amazing. That I'm beautiful. That he couldn't believe how beautiful I was when he first saw me in his kitchen... And somehow, the sound of his voice begins coaxing me into forgetting there's a very large dick moving inside me.

"You okay?"

"Mmm hmm."

"Does it feel good?"

"It feels...okay," I answer honestly. "But not bad."

"I'll slow down a bit."

"No, no, I'm getting used to it. Are you *really* big?"

"You'll appreciate it later."

I take a deep breath. "Just do whatever's normal at times like this. Not too crazy, but normal."

Tyler begins gyrating on top of me with a tad more enthusiasm, and I'm shocked to feel my pelvis instinctively begin moving and gyrating in synchronicity with his.

"That's good," he whispers. "Nice."

After a moment, Tyler makes a sound that tells me he's *really* enjoying what he's feeling, and the sound of his obvious pleasure flips a switch inside me. I grab his ass tightly and revel in the feeling of his muscles tensing and releasing on top of me.

"Holy fuck," he chokes out. He thrusts deeply into me—so deep he makes my eyes pop out. And then I feel a rippling sensation inside of me. And then stillness. He sighs. "Lord have mercy on my soul."

For a long moment, we're both quiet, except for the sound of our mutual ragged breathing.

I feel the warmth of his skin against mine.

Smell his scent.

Hear the perfect song he selected for this moment, playing on a loop.

I sigh. "And, just like that, you're a lifelong memory, Tyler Caldwell."

He kisses my cheek. "Don't judge sex by that—and certainly don't judge sex with *me* by that. That was just, you know, step one. It's gonna get better and better, I promise."

"So how soon will you be ready to do it again? Five

minutes? Tomorrow? How does this work?"

He chuckles. "I'll be ready to go again in about an hour. And probably once more after that. Either way, my eager little beaver, I promise you're not leaving this house tonight until I've fucked you good and right."

CHAPTER FIFTEEN

Tyler pulls his motorcycle to a stop in front of my dorm building in the predawn darkness. I reluctantly unwrap my arms from around his leather jacket, slide off the back of his bike, and take off the helmet he gave me to wear. Tyler's UCLA sweatshirt is mammoth on me. I hug it to me, reveling in the softness of the fleece against my flesh and the deliciousness of Tyler's scent wafting up from the fabric.

I feel drugged. High on life. High on Tyler. On his skin. His smile. His tongue. His laugh. I feel intoxicated by our night together, especially that incredible third time we had sex tonight. "Now I know what all the fuss is about," I said to Tyler after that third time, and he laughed.

Tyler pulls off his helmet and kills the motor on his bike. "So I'll see you tonight around eight?" he says.

"I'll be there with bells on," I say. "And hard nipples."

He laughs again. *God, I love his laugh.* "You had fun tonight?" he asks.

"Best night ever."

"Just imagine if I would have fucked you at the party the way I fucked you that third time."

"I just didn't know what I didn't know."

Tyler bites his lip. "Well, now you know, little freshman."

"I sure do." I hold up three fingers. "Three times."

"I knew you'd be a little vixen once you got comfortable. But I had no idea you'd get *that* comfortable *that* fast. That third time, you went full-throttle sex kitten on me. *Damn.*"

I giggle. "I can't wait to do it again. I feel addicted."

We linger for a bit, cooing at each other, giggling, whispering, neither of us wanting this magical night to end. Finally, I pull myself from his soft lips and intoxicating scent and glide on air through the front entrance of my dorm building. Once inside, I forego the elevator in favor of the stairs, just because I'm so happy to be alive. What a night!

I reach the door to my room and open it slowly, not wanting to wake Clarissa. But when I step inside the darkened room, I'm shocked to see what appears to be two intertwined bodies gyrating on Clarissa's bed.

"Gah!" I blurt, spinning around and bonking my forehead smack into the door. "Ouch! Sorry! *Gah.*"

"It's fine, Zooey," Clarissa says softly behind me. "It's just Dimitri. We're fully clothed."

I turn around. My eyes have adjusted now, and I can plainly see Dimitri and Clarissa lying, clothed, on top of her small bed.

"Hi, Dimitri."

"Hi," Dimitri replies sheepishly. "Sorry I'm here. I meant to be gone before you got back. We were watching a movie and I fell asleep."

"And then you woke up," Clarissa says suggestively.

"And then I woke up," Dimitri agrees, his tone equally suggestive. He kisses Clarissa on her cheek and pops up from the bed. "I'll text you later."

"You'd better."

"I take it things went well with Tyler?" Dimitri says to me. "After the way he lost his shit about you today on campus, I figured he'd turn on the charm."

"It went great." I exchange a loaded look with Clarissa. "He's sweet."

"Yeah? Glad to hear it. He's got a rep for being a bit of a cocky dick sometimes, actually."

"Not at all. He's wonderful. He made me dinner. We did our homework. Made out a little. I'm seeing him again tomorrow night. Well, actually, tonight, I guess. We're assigned to work on two class projects together, so we'll be seeing a lot of each other this quarter."

"Cool." Dimitri heads toward the door. "If he's ever a dick to you, though, let me know. I'll beat him up for you."

Clarissa and I giggle.

"Oh, hey, Dimitri," I say. "I almost forgot. Tyler and I have to do some experiments for Social Psych, and we were wondering if you'd help us out?" I explain briefly what we're planning to do, and both Clarissa and Dimitri say they'd be happy to assist us.

Finally, Dimitri leaves and Clarissa immediately leaps out of her bed, her face aglow.

"Did you and Tyler do it?" she asks.

"Three times."

Clarissa squeals. "My little girl's all grown up! And? Was Tyler's T-shirt truth in advertising?"

"One hundred percent. He was a sex god, Clarissa. I

couldn't have picked a better de-virginizer if I searched the world over." I sigh happily. "Tonight was sheer perfection."

We plop ourselves down onto Clarissa's bed, and I proceed to regale her with details of the night, and she oohs and aahs and squeals enthusiastically throughout my story. When I'm done talking, Clarissa tells me about how she and Dimitri hooked up tonight to "watch a movie"...and how midway through the opening credits that nerd shocked her by taking her into his arms and kissing the heck out of her.

"So are the rumors about nerds true?" I ask.

"I don't know yet," Clarissa says. "We just made out. But it was *really* hot and heavy. I've got high hopes it's going to be damned good when it happens."

"Oh, Dimitri's been promoted from an 'if' to a 'when'?"

"Definitely. But enough about me. I want to hear more about you and Tyler. Do you truly think you can handle sleeping with him for five whole weeks?"

"Well, if you mean will I die of sheer pleasure after five weeks with him, that's a very real possibility."

"No, I mean do you think you'll be able to handle being his friend and nothing more after the five weeks are up?"

"Oh, *that*." I bite the inside of my cheek. "Yeah, I think... Hmm." I twist my lips, deep in thought. "Can I ask you something, Clarissa? When you had all that mind-blowing sex with that basketball player douchebag in high school, was there ever a moment when you felt like maybe you were falling for him? Not all the time, just when you were in the midst of pure ecstasy and—"

"No."

"Hang on. I mean, not in real life, but when you were in the throes of ecstasy, and your toes were curling, and his voice was in your ear, and he smelled so good, and everything he did turned you on, did you ever think—"

"*No.* Not once, Zooey. Never did I ever think, even for a nanosecond, I might be falling for the douchebag."

My stomach drops into my toes. "Oh."

"You think you're falling for Tyler?"

I shake my head. But then slowly nod. "Maybe?" I sigh. "I think if I'm not careful here, I'm in serious danger of turning into a Stage Five Clinger on him. Like, seriously."

Clarissa twists her mouth. "Then I guess you'd better be careful, huh?"

I flap my lips together. "Crap."

CHAPTER SIXTEEN

"A syllabus?" I ask incredulously, staring at the type-written paper Tyler just handed me.

Tyler's eyes are sparkling. "I didn't want to risk forgetting something important."

I look down at the paper again.

SYLLABUS

The Miseducation of Zooey Cartwright

Instructor: Tyler Caldwell

Student: Zooey Cartwright

Course Objective: The complete sexual education and satisfaction of Miss Zooey Cartwright aka Eager Beaver.

Course Length: Five Weeks

The body of the document is broken up into two phases, each containing a laundry list of line items. In Phase One, the "suggested but not required" course topics are listed as:

Beginning Sexual Positions

Beginning Sexual Locations

The Art of the Blow Job

Zooey Gets Good at Getting Off During Oral

Zooey Gets Off During Intercourse!

Extra Credit: Zooey Gets Off While Giving Head

I look up from the paper again. "You've put some thought into this."

"That's the understatement of the century."

My crotch is tingling. "How long do you think Phase One will last?"

"I don't know. I've never done this before. We'll just have to play it by ear. Do you have any questions about Phase One before we move on?"

"Beginning Sexual Locations?"

"Bed, shower, chair, floor, against the wall. Maybe the backseat of a car if I can borrow one."

I laugh. "I thought you meant beginning sexual locations *on my body*." I point to my mouth and crotch, and Tyler bursts out laughing.

"Yeah, that, too. Advanced sexual locations *on your body* will be part of Phase Two. If we get to Phase Two, of course."

"*If* we get there?"

"Three nights a week for five weeks is only fifteen nights. Not that many times together, if you think about it. I don't expect us to get through the entire syllabus. I just listed everything I could think of, just in case you turn out to be a quick study."

I feel crestfallen. I hadn't put it together that our five weeks together will actually only amount to fifteen nights. "I don't want to miss out on something exciting simply because we run out of time," I say. "I want to do it all, Tyler."

He grins. "Maybe you should hold off on making a proclamation like that until *after* you've read Phase Two."

I return to the paper in my hand and silently read the items listed under Phase Two.

Advanced Sexual Positions

Advanced Sexual Locations

Hello, Zooey's G-spot!

Dirty Fun with Food

"Oh, No, I Hope Nobody Catches Us Fucking!"

Role-Play

Toys

Extra Credit: TBD

I look up from the sheet of paper, adrenaline coursing through my veins.

"You still want to do it all?" Tyler asks.

"Absolutely."

Tyler's eyes ignite. "You don't have any questions about any of it?"

I look at the paper again. It's shaking in my hand. "I'm not even sure what all this stuff refers to, to be honest. What's TBD?"

"To be determined."

"Yeah, I know that, but what does it refer to here?"

"I'll tell you if we get there."

I gaze at the list for another moment. "You know what? Surprise me. As long as you keep getting yeses from me along the way, then I'm good." I crumple the syllabus into a ball and throw it across the room. "You lead and I'll follow, Tyler Caldwell."

Tyler's eyes ignite. "I think you might be perfect."

"Can I put in one small request, though? Teeny tiny. Can you teach me 'The Art of the Blow Job' first? I had a dream last night I was giving you a blow job, and when I woke up, I was kind of...*fluttering* down there."

Tyler's facial expression morphs into one of pure arousal. "My pleasure." He stands and pulls me up from his couch. "I take my duty as your sex educator very seriously, Zooey Cartwright. If my student has a *thirst* for a particular knowledge, then by God, I'm going to *quench* her particular thirst."

CHAPTER SEVENTEEN

Tyler's sitting naked on the edge of his bed. I'm kneeling naked between his legs, listening to him explain what I should—and absolutely should *not*—do while giving him a blow job.

"But, really, once you've got those basic techniques down, the most important thing is enthusiasm," Tyler says. "You can use all the 'right techniques' until you're blue in the face, but if you're not genuinely enjoying sucking my dick—if you're not *savoring* the taste of my cock in your mouth and aching to get me off simply because doing it gets *you* off—then it's gonna be a perfunctory blow job at best. And blow jobs should never, ever be *perfunctory*, sweetheart." He grimaces.

"I had no idea there was such a thing as anything other than a totally awesome blow job," I say. "I thought every time a girl puts a guy's dick in her mouth, it's heaven."

"Nope. It's the same thing for girls with oral, or so I've been told. I know you've got no basis of comparison, but one day you'll find out I'm a genius at carpet munching. Probably the best you'll ever have."

"Well, that's a bummer. You're saying it's all downhill from here?"

"Sorry to say, yes. I'm supernaturally gifted at eating pussy."

"So what's your secret? Enthusiasm?"

"Yup. I love doing it. When I eat it, I *savor* it like I'll never get the privilege of doing it again. I savor it like I've discovered the fountain of youth between a girl's legs. And I must say your beautiful pussy is particularly tasty. Tastiest one yet, for sure."

I swallow hard. Man, he's turning me on.

"Honestly," Tyler continues. "I can't teach you to be gifted at sucking dick. Geniuses are born, not made. I can only teach you the techniques to make you exceptionally *good* at sucking dick. But that's no small thing. I'll never in my life complain about an exceptionally *good* blow job. But a *supernatural* blow job? A mind-blowing one?" He kisses his fingertips like a chef. "That's fine *art*."

I giggle. "So you're an *arteest*?"

"And my medium is pussy."

We both laugh.

"All right. You ready to give it a whirl, sweetheart?"

I nod.

He puts his hand on the top of my head. "Bon appétit, baby. Make my cock your art. Just, please, eager beaver, don't forget the number one rule I told you. Beavers should never, ever use their teeth to gnaw on the big log."

Approximately four minutes later...

Tyler's fingers rake urgently across my scalp. "Oh, fuck yeah," he grits out. "Now suck just a little bit harder, baby. Oh, yeah. Just like that. That's perfect. Keep doing that. *Don't stop.*" His cock twitches sharply in my mouth. His fingers are gripping the top of my bobbing head. "Now touch yourself with your free hand."

I slide my free hand between my legs while continuing to grope him with the other.

"You've got the hang of it now, baby," Tyler whispers. "Oh, fuck. This is getting good." He groans loudly and shoves himself farther into my mouth.

I look up at his face. He looks like he's on the cusp of complete ecstasy. And, all of a sudden, I feel *empowered*. I might be the one on my knees here, but I'm suddenly realizing I'm in charge. I've got this boy's manhood between my teeth, after all. Not to mention his balls in the palm of my hand. He's at my mercy, quite literally. *And I love it.*

Excitement floods me. I increase the intensity of my assault, adding a little extra flair to the movement of my tongue. My hand moves from Tyler's balls to his hard ass and into his crack. I slip a fingertip inside him, exactly the way Tyler suggested I do if I was feeling it, and Tyler goes freaking crazy on me.

"I'm gonna come," he blurts.

I slip my finger farther inside him, making sure he knows who's running the show here.

"Oh, fuck, I'm gonna come so fucking hard," he grits out. "Into your mouth."

I nod enthusiastically while continuing to work myself with my free hand.

Tyler yanks sharply on my hair. Pushes himself into my mouth. "Swallow me down, Zooey."

"Mmm hmm."

He makes a sound that makes my skin prick and my toes curl. And then it happens. *Nirvana.* Warm, salty liquid gushes into my mouth as waves of pleasure begin seizing my clit and everything connected to it. I swallow Tyler down and yank my mouth off his hard-on, consumed by the pleasure of my own climax.

Finally, after my body stops clenching, I look up at Tyler, licking my lips. "I came," I say simply. I smile proudly.

Tyler strokes my hair. "Well, I'll be damned. Who would have guessed my eager little beaver would turn out to be fucking Van Gogh."

CHAPTER EIGHTEEN

It's Wednesday night. Well, actually, the wee hours of Thursday morning. And for the third night in a row, Tyler's dropping me off in front of my dorm after yet another amazing night together. Tonight's activities? Well, sex, of course. In a variety of positions and locations in his bedroom. On his desk. On his bed. On the floor. We also watched a little porn. That was kind of odd. And in between all that, we also worked on our Shakespeare project. Fleshed out our Social Psych experiments. Oh, and then I sat on Tyler's face.

And now, here we are, once again. He's straddling his motorcycle with the engine off, wearing a T-shirt that reads Maintain Swagger at All Times. I'm wrapped in Tyler's soft sweatshirt, kissing him goodbye and feeling like I'm floating on a cloud.

Tyler pulls out of our kiss and lets out a long, mournful sigh.

"What?" I ask.

Tyler slides his palm on my cheek and rests his forehead against mine. "What am I gonna do with you?"

"Anything you want. Literally. Please. As soon as possible."

He laughs. "You're enjoying your miseducation, are you, eager beaver?"

I want to tell him the word "enjoyment" doesn't come close to encapsulating what I'm feeling right now. That I feel addicted to having sex with him. To just *being* with him. To simply gazing at him. I want to tell him he makes me laugh—that I'm not normally *this* giggly, I swear. I want to tell him he makes me swoon. And flutter. And feel like I can do anything I set my mind to. But I don't dare say any of it. The last thing I want to do is make Tyler think I've morphed into a Stage Five Clinger, especially this fast. "Yes, I'm enjoying my miseducation a lot, professor," I reply.

Tyler sighs again. "It's not that I don't *want* to see you again before Monday. It's that I can't figure out how to make it happen."

Well, that came out of left field. He said that like we were in the middle of a conversation about seeing each other before Monday—like I'd *asked* to see him again before then. But, um, unless I'm having a psychotic breakdown, I'm pretty sure I didn't say a word about that. "You told me right from the start we'd be seeing each other on Monday through Wednesday," I say. "I have zero expectation of seeing you otherwise."

"If we were playing a home game this week, I could *maybe* squeeze in some time to see you on Friday. But this week's game is in Texas, and we're traveling on Friday. And Sundays are my only day to rest up, catch up on my reading. My roommates and I go out to breakfast together on Sundays and then hang out and watch football. It's our thing. Relaxing on Sundays is sacred to me."

I'm flabbergasted. What on earth have I said or done to make him think he needs to explain all this to me? "Tyler, I'm super busy, too," I say. "Freshman theater majors are basically slave labor for the mainstage production. I've got to build and paint sets and sew costumes for, like, fifteen hours a week. I've got a research paper due for History of Theater. A bunch of reading for Anthropology. Plus, I'm going to a couple parties this weekend and—"

"Parties?"

I cock my head to the side. What on earth am I seeing in his face? He looks tense. "Yeah, a dorm party on Friday night. It's a pizza-and-movie-night thing to help us get to know each other. And then a theater party on Saturday night. I'm going with a couple girls I met in slave labor. Oh, and Clarissa and I are going to Dimitri's on Saturday afternoon to watch your game with him and his roommates."

"Who's throwing the theater party?"

I bite my lip. Is he...*jealous*? Is that what I'm seeing in his face? "This guy who's starring in the mainstage production. *Hamlet*. I guess the guy is the Tyler Caldwell of the theater department. Everyone says he'll be a huge star one day. One to watch." I somehow keep myself from smiling. I'm telling him the truth about all of that, actually. No exaggeration whatsoever. But that doesn't make it any less fun to say in this moment, when Tyler's so clearly not pleased to hear it.

"Cool," Tyler says, but his jaw is clenched. He takes a deep breath. Bites his lip. Furrows his brow. He looks like he's hosting a wrestling match inside his brain. "Hey, will you do me a favor? Text me Saturday morning before my game and wish me luck? My dad and sister always do that for me on game days. It always helps me get my 'Tyler Caldwell' going if

I know certain people are watching."

"Your 'Tyler Caldwell'? You're referring to yourself in third person now? Not good, babe."

He smiles. "Just on game days. I think of myself as this kind of Tyler Caldwell machine on game days. So will you text me?"

I try to keep myself from smiling too big at this latest surprise. I've been assuming texting would be off-limits on our days off from each other. I figured me texting Tyler would make him feel smothered.

"Sure," I say casually. "I'll text 'Tyler Caldwell' on game day. No problem."

"Well, I mean, not just on game day," he says. "Feel free to text me any day. Check in. Say hi. I mean, don't light up my phone like crazy or turn into a stalker on me, but don't be a stranger."

I cock my head to the side again, trying to understand the bizarreness that is Tyler Caldwell. He looks tortured right now. "I'll try," I say. "But don't be offended if I'm pretty much MIA until Monday. Like I said, I'm going to be pretty busy the next few days."

Tyler squints at me like he's trying to decide if I'm pulling his leg or not.

I remain stone-faced. "But feel free to text *me* if you're thinking about me or want to say hi. I mean, don't light up my phone like crazy or anything—like I said, I'm going to be really busy. But, yeah, feel free to text me *occasionally* to say hello. But don't stalk me."

We stare at each other for a long moment.

Tyler grins. "I'll be sure to text you," he says. "I mean, not too much. I wouldn't want you thinking I'm a Stage Five Clinger or anything."

"God, no. Text me just enough to let me know you're thinking of me. Not too much to scare me off." I wink.

"Got it," he says. He bites his lip again. "Okay, my little beaver. Have fun the next few days discovering the joys of college life. Just promise me you won't do shots, okay? It's too damned easy to get shitfaced from shots and make terrible decisions."

"Thanks, Dad. But I don't drink. No need to worry about me."

Tyler breathes a sigh of relief. "Good. Neither do I. At least, not during the season."

"You said you were drunk the night I met you."

"Oh, yeah. That was the exception, not the rule for me. Once in a blue moon." He pulls me to him and nuzzles my nose. "Hey, make sure you get plenty of sleep this weekend, okay? I've got all sorts of exciting plans for your hot little body for Monday night, and you'll need to be ready to go all night."

I salute him. "I'll be ready, sir. See you on Monday in Social Psych."

"See you then. I can't wait."

"I'll be counting the days," I whisper.

"Hours. Minutes."

My heart skips a beat. But, somehow, I manage to keep my composure and play it cool. "Okay, well, I'll see you Monday, Tyler," I say calmly. "Have a great game on Saturday. I'll be sure to text 'Tyler Caldwell' and wish him luck." I give him a soft kiss on his cheek. "Thanks for a great three nights this week. I'll never forget them."

CHAPTER NINETEEN

I don't want to be here. I *should* want to be here, but I don't. And that pisses me off. This is what I've wanted since I got my acceptance letter to UCLA—to be at a loud, crazy theater party on a Saturday night, surrounded by people who spontaneously burst into show tunes while standing around concocting imaginary rap battles between Shakespeare and Arthur Miller. And yet, now that I'm here, all I can think about is how much I'd rather be lying naked with Tyler Caldwell. Well, actually *underneath* Tyler Caldwell, to be more exact.

Gah! I'm pathetic. Clingy and gross and pathetic! How have I become this smitten this fast? I absolutely hate clingy, pathetic, obsessed girls, and now I'm one of them! I need to stop this right now. I need to be present and in the moment and stop yearning to be with someone right now I'll be seeing a mere two days from now. *Get a grip, Zooey!*

Thankfully, I haven't been sexed up and smitten like this nonstop for the past few days. To the contrary, I've been so busy with my classes and meeting new people and exploring campus, I've hardly thought about Tyler at all. Okay, that's a lie. I've thought about Tyler a ton, but it's been manageable. Within the zone of reasonableness.

But all that reasonableness flew out the window this

afternoon the minute I saw Tyler playing football. I saw him on that field on TV, decked out in his pads and helmet and tight little pants, terrorizing Texas A&M's running backs and receivers like a freaking warlord, and all hell broke loose inside me. *An obsession was born.*

Frankly, it's not my fault I'm feeling this way. I was raised on football. It's in my blood. And Tyler was magnificent today. He was graceful. Fast. Savage. Powerful. A panther stalking his prey. A freight train on the tackle. Not to mention a bit of a thug at times, too. Which was hot as all get-out. When anyone disrespected or offensively interfered with Tyler—or, God forbid, blocked him in his back—he wasn't restrained about communicating his displeasure. He bumped the offender's chest with his. Chewed his opponent out like the dude had just murdered a puppy. At one point, when an opposing player got in Tyler's face right after administering a questionable block on him, Tyler lurched at the guy so fiercely, Tyler's teammates had to physically hold him back. Of course, Tyler quickly pulled himself together after that incident and got his head back in the game. But it was too late for me. I'd seen the raw, primal side of Tyler—the forest fire raging inside him—*and I liked what I saw.* Indeed, I liked it a lot.

Seeing Tyler play football for the first time made me feel exactly the way I did when my grandparents took me to see *Wicked* for the first time in New York. *My very soul burst into flames of desire.* And so, I shot off a text to Tyler, right then and there while sitting on Dimitri's couch, even though I knew Tyler wouldn't see my message until hours later:

Watching you play football is making this eager

beaver's beaver extremely wet. Can't wait to see you on Monday. Get ready because I'm going to attack you.

A friend of mine from the theater department says something to me, drawing my attention away from my thoughts of Tyler and back to the party.

"I'm sorry?" I say.

"I'm going to the kitchen for a beer. You want anything?"

"A water would be great," I reply. "Thanks."

As my friend departs, I pull out my phone and check to see if Tyler's replied to my naughty message yet. But, nope. The only texts between Tyler and me are the unanswered trio from me to him from throughout the day. My text from this morning, wishing Tyler luck in the game, my sext about my extremely wet beaver sent to Tyler during the game, and a third text sent from me to Tyler right after the game, congratulating him on the team's win and his forced fumble.

Crap. I shouldn't have sent Tyler *three* unanswered texts in a row. If that doesn't scream "clingy," then I don't know what does. *Shoot.* I should have continued to play it cool with Tyler, the way I did when he dropped me off the other night. I should have wished him luck in the game, the thing he specifically asked me to do, and left it at that. *Rookie mistake, Zooey!*

"Hey, aren't you in my History of Theater class?" a male voice asks, pulling me out of my thoughts. The figure standing before me is a cute guy from my class. David, I think his name is.

"Yeah. Hi. I'm Zooey."

"Dylan."

David. Dylan. Close enough.

"Are you a theater major?" I ask. "Or just getting your arts requirement out of the way?"

"Theater major," he says.

I quickly assess him. He's cute. Fit. Not a guy I'd peg for a theater major at all. He looks like a classic California surfer dude.

"So have you picked your topic for the research paper yet?" Dylan asks.

"I think so." I tell him my idea for the paper. In return, he tells me about his research topic, and I feign listening. Honestly, I don't care. I can't stop thinking about how I came on too strong with Tyler today. What if Tyler feels smothered and decides he doesn't want to continue with my miseducation for the full five weeks? Oh, man, just the thought makes me feel panicky.

My phone buzzes, and I pull it out of my pocket like a hot potato as Dylan continues talking. It's a text from Tyler.

Your beaver still wet for me, eager beaver?

My heartrate spikes.

Yes.

I'm too excited to manage anything wittier than that.

I just landed in LA. Where are you?

"Excuse me," I blurt to Dylan, cutting him off midsentence. I hold up my phone by way of explanation. "I've got to..." But I don't bother finishing my sentence. I sprint around a corner

132

into a hallway, my chest heaving with excitement, and tap out a quick reply.

At a theater party.

Address?

Why? You want to hang out with a bunch of theater majors?

No. I want to pick you up wherever you are and bring you back to my house and fuck your brains out.

I gasp and look up from my phone, adrenaline flooding me. What the hell happened to the guy who couldn't possibly see me on any days besides Monday through Wednesday? I'm dying to ask Tyler that very question, but I force myself not to look a gift horse in the mouth. I text the address of the party to Tyler and add lamely...

Thank you.

Tyler replies instantly.

Don't thank me. I'm not coming to get you for your benefit. I'm coming to get you for mine.

CHAPTER TWENTY

In a frenzy of heat, Tyler pulls off my clothes and guides me onto his kitchen table on my back and begins covering my body with greedy kisses. His lips are on my neck and then my breast. My nipple is in his hungry mouth. His fingers are brushing lightly against my thigh and then across my hipbone. I arch my back with pleasure at the urgency of his touch, his mouth, his lips.

"Your roommates might come in," I whisper.

"They're all out getting postgame pussy," he says. "We've got at least a couple hours."

"Oh, no," I gasp out. "I hope nobody catches us fucking!" It's a reference to one of the line items under Phase Two of Tyler's syllabus, of course. But I'm also being sincere: If any of his roommates were to catch us in the act, I'd die of embarrassment on the spot.

"No one will catch us," Tyler growls. "But if they did, it'd be hot as fuck."

He takes off his shirt, revealing not only his usual hotness but also several horrific-looking welts and bruises on his glorious torso—mementos from the bone-crushing hits he administered in today's game, no doubt.

"Tyler," I breathe. "You poor thing."

"A taste of your pussy and the pain will magically disappear."

He opens my legs forcefully, nothing like the gentle way he's opened my legs this past week—and my entire body spasms at this new kind of touch. His tongue finds my clit. Again, his urgency is something new. I arch my back, shoving myself into him fervently. He groans loudly, obviously enjoying my enthusiasm, and the sound of his pleasure sends me over the edge. I let out a low moan as my body begins clenching and rippling into his mouth, and he responds with an animalistic sound that sends shivers across my skin.

By the time my climax has subsided, Tyler's got a condom stretched onto his massive erection. He pulls a chair out from the kitchen table, sits, and guides me to straddle him. For a brief moment, I stand over him, gawking at his hard-on straining toward my entrance. Every fiber of my body wants to lower myself onto it, but my brain is hesitating. That thing looks like it could impale me.

"You're gonna love it on top," he says, reading my mind. "Trust me."

Well, that's good enough for me. Because I *do* trust Tyler. Completely. I position myself over his tip, and he grabs my hips and pushes me down onto him.

I gasp at the sensation of him filling me at this new angle. Oh, man, he's deeper inside me than he's ever been. He's taking my breath away.

"Breathe," Tyler whispers. "Relax into it."

I do as I'm told, and my body molds to him comfortably.

"Now ride me," he commands. He grabs the back of my

neck. "Hump me, back and forth. Snap your hips and rub your clit against my dick as you ride me."

I follow his instructions and, instantly, my body explodes with pleasure. "*Oh.*"

"Good?"

"Really good."

I hump him until we're both in a frenzy.

"I'm gonna slide my thumb up your ass now," Tyler grits out. His voice is husky with desire. "Keep riding me, cowgirl."

I never thought the idea of Tyler or anyone sticking a thumb or anything else up my ass would turn me on, but I'll be damned, I'm enthralled by the idea. I nod.

"Yes?"

"Yes," I gasp.

His thumb enters me and pushes gently past the thick ring of muscles at my entrance. I gasp at the unexpectedly pleasurable sensation and begin riding him even harder, my body flooded with a new kind of pleasure.

After a moment, Tyler does...something...back there. What the hell is he doing in my ass? And all of a sudden, I'm so freaking turned on, I can't control my body. I feel like he's just slammed his foot down onto my body's gas pedal.

"Holy shit," Tyler chokes out. "Someone likes ass play."

I'm wailing with pleasure. Screaming Tyler's name. Suddenly, I feel like my eyes are about to roll back into my head.

And then...

A supernatural stillness overtakes me. Time stops. My skin erupts with goose bumps. My toes curl.

Heaven.

Shockwaves of pleasure shoot through my every nerve ending, all at once, zinging into my toes and fingertips and clit and ass with unyielding force. I jerk around for a moment on top of Tyler like a sinner at a Baptist revival, until finally, blessedly, I throw my arms around his neck and collapse into a sweaty pile of goo.

Tyler wraps his powerful arms around my back and pulls me close—so close, my breasts smash into his chest. "That was amazing," he whispers, his breathing labored. "The best sex I've ever had."

I take a deep breath, trying to steady my racing heart. "For me, too."

"That statement means absolutely nothing coming from you, Zooey."

I giggle. "What the hell just happened? I felt like I was possessed by a demon."

Tyler kisses my bare shoulder. "That, my dear, was your first all-body orgasm. Ten times more powerful than a clitoral orgasm. The holy grail."

"It felt amazing."

"For me, too. I've never felt a G-spot orgasm from the inside before. I've only made it happen with my fingers until you." He sighs contentedly. "God, that felt incredible. The minute you started squeezing my cock so hard, I lost it."

I bite his ear lobe and press myself into him. "*I want to do it again.*"

"Oh, you will, eager beaver. I'll order you a G-spot vibrator online so you can practice and get good at it. That way, it'll become second nature for you."

I nuzzle his nose. "I don't want a vibrator. I want *you*."

"Sweetheart, you want a vibrator. Whenever we're apart, I want you to use it. The better you get at getting yourself off from your G-spot, the more you'll get off from my cock when we fuck. Think of it like training for game day."

I bite his earlobe again. "Okay, coach. Whatever you say. Get me a vibrator. Get me a thousand vibrators." I grab his cheeks and press my forehead against his. I feel unleashed. "Just as long as you do that thing to me again one more time tonight."

He smiles. "Sorry, baby. Not tonight. I played football and traveled today, remember? I'm wiped. There's a reason I pulled you on top of me. I can barely move."

I pull back slightly, suddenly feeling like an insensitive idiot. "I'm so sorry. Do you need ice or something?"

"Yeah, actually. There are ice packs in the freezer. Thanks."

I clamber off him and bound to the freezer, my pulse pounding in my ears. "No wonder you said you need to rest up on Sundays. You poor thing." I hand him a couple of icepacks and begin scooping my clothes off the floor. "No need to drive me home tonight. I'll call the late-night campus service so you can crash."

"Zooey, don't be lame. You've misunderstood me."

I abruptly stop picking up my clothes and stare at him blankly.

"I was hoping you'd crash here tonight. With me."

I'm astonished. "You want me to spend the night here?"

"Yeah. I was thinking maybe I could persuade you to kiss my bruises for me before I fall asleep." He smiles. "And then when I wake up in the morning, I promise I'll turn you into a demon again."

My mouth is hanging open.

"I've got an extra toothbrush," Tyler adds quickly, apparently feeling the need to further argue his point. "And you can wear one of my T-shirts to sleep in, if you want. Unless you'd prefer to sleep naked. No argument from me there."

I'm floored. It's one thing for Tyler to want to have a little postgame sex with me on a Saturday night, but now he wants me to spend the night?

"So will you stay?" Tyler asks.

I feel the urge to jump for joy, but I manage to keep my cool. "It depends. Which of your T-shirts would you loan me to wear?"

"Well, unfortunately, I don't own a T-shirt that says Phase Two Is My Bitch! So I guess I'll have to settle for the one that says Hot as Fuck. If you in that shirt isn't an elephant wearing an elephant T-shirt, then I don't know what is."

If he blew on me, I'd tip over. "Great," I say. "And don't worry, I'll get my morning nookie tomorrow and head right out. I've got lots of homework to do."

"Well, there's no need to rush off. My roommates and I get breakfast at this diner in the Village every Sunday. You should come. I mean, you've got to eat, right?"

What on earth happened to the guy who said doing his own thing on Sundays is "sacred" to him? I nod. "I love breakfast. Most important meal of the day."

"Absolutely. And you don't need to rush off after breakfast, either. Sundays are all about resting up, watching a little football, catching up on homework. There's no reason you can't hang out and do all that with me. You can do whatever homework you've got while I'm doing mine."

I'm stupefied. Mind-fucked beyond comprehension. Is he punking me? "Great," I say cautiously. "Why don't we work on our class projects tomorrow for a bit, too? I've noticed we've been spending a disproportionate amount of time on our 'miseducation project' while neglecting the other two. Not that I'm complaining about that, mind you." I snicker.

"You know what? You're totally right. We've absolutely been neglecting our class projects. Totally irresponsible of us. Inexcusable." He gets up gingerly from his chair, his angry bruises and welts making me grimace for him, and tosses his used condom into a trash can. "Come on, Zooey Cartwright. Time for us to crash. It's the only responsible thing to do, after all. Crash tonight and work on our class projects tomorrow." He flashes me a cocky grin. "As anyone will tell you, baby, I'm nothing if not responsible."

CHAPTER TWENTY-ONE

After sex this morning in yet another new position—let's just say this cowgirl enthusiastically earned her "reverse spurs" this morning—I'm now sitting in a diner with Tyler and his five roommates, watching them scarf down enough eggs, pancakes, and bacon to feed at least fifteen people. Not even exaggerating.

"Okay, it's official," Tyler says, putting his coffee mug down with a thud. "Zooey Cartwright will laugh at anything."

"No," Aaron shoots back defensively. "Zooey Cartwright laughed because I'm a comedic genius."

"That was the stupidest joke I've ever heard," Tyler says.

"It was just too sophisticated for your feeble mind to comprehend, dude."

Tyler laughs.

"Too many *cheetahs*," Aaron says slowly by way of explanation. He's repeating his punchline from a moment ago. "It's why the animals were expelled from the zoo. Get it, Tyler? Because 'cheetahs' sounds like 'cheaters.' It's a *pun*."

"That's pretty high-concept stuff, Heckerling."

"I know. Don't feel bad if it sailed right over your head, bro. You can't help it if you were born with a tiny brain."

I giggle again, every bit as much as I did when Aaron first

told that stupid joke a minute ago. Only this time, I'm not laughing at Aaron, but at Tyler. Specifically, at the deadpan expression on his gorgeous face. At this point, Tyler could read his grocery list and I'd laugh.

Tyler turns his mocking wrath on me. "Is Aaron paying you to laugh at his stupid jokes, Zooey? Tell the truth."

I shake my head. "It's his delivery more than what he says. Aaron is just inherently funny."

"Traitor!" Tyler barks at me, but his eyes are full of warmth. "Don't encourage him, Zooey. Heckerling already thinks he's the funniest guy on the team, even though we all know it's *me*."

"Ha!" Aaron says.

"It's true. I'm way funnier than you," Tyler insists. "In fact, I'm funnier than *all* of you lunkheads. Zooey's only been laughing at your lame jokes all breakfast long because she's from the Midwest and Midwestern girls are raised to be extra polite. Isn't that right, Zooey? You're just a sweet Midwestern girl who doesn't want your new friends to feel bad they're not as funny as me?"

"I genuinely think everyone's hilarious. Especially Aaron."

"Ha!" Aaron says. "I knew I liked you, Zooey Cartwright."

"This is total bullshit and I can prove it," Tyler says defiantly. "Okay, guys, here's what we're gonna do. Each of you has one minute to make Zooey Cartwright laugh. You succeed in your mission, I'll give you ten bucks. You fail, *Zooey* will get the ten bucks, instead. With cash on the line, we ought to find out who here is 'hilarious' and who's just being polite."

"Why would you make that bet?" Aaron asks Tyler.

"You're on the paying end of it either way."

"Some things are more valuable to me than money, son," Tyler replies with mock solemnity. He turns to me. "You think you can bottle up that cute little giggle of yours long enough to earn yourself fifty bucks, giggler?"

I zip my mouth. "You'll never hear my 'cute little giggle' again." I'm telling the truth about that, by the way. God as my witness, wild horses couldn't make me laugh for the next five minutes. I want that money.

Approximately three and a half minutes later...

"You suck," Tyler says to me.

"I suck," I agree, flapping my lips together. "I thought I'd be so much better at this." I grasp the one measly ten-dollar bill I managed to win thanks to Hanalei and look around the table at Tyler's other four roommates—all of whom are now triumphantly holding ten-dollar bills.

"How lame is Hanalei, though," Aaron says. "If you can't make Zooey Cartwright laugh, then you're clearly as funny as paint drying."

"Hanalei just took pity on me," I say. I look at Hanalei. "You threw the game out of pity, didn't you?"

"Nope, I'm a competitive bastard," Hanalei replies in his deep baritone voice. "I'd never throw any game, no matter what." But he winks at me, telling me I've guessed right.

"Okay, Tyler," Aaron says. "Your turn now. But let's make this a bit more interesting, shall we? I've got *thirty* bucks that says you can't make Zooey Cartwright laugh within thirty seconds."

"*Thirty seconds?* You all got a full minute."

"Yeah, but you've got a huge advantage over all of us," Aaron retorts. "You and Zooey haven't stopped making googly eyes at each other since we sat down. Odds are high she'll laugh her ass off if you so much as smile at the girl."

I feel my cheeks coloring. Tyler and I have been making googly eyes at each other?

Aaron and Tyler haggle for a bit and finally reach agreement about the game.

"Okay, okay." Tyler says. He snaps his fingers at me. "Zooey Cartwright! Pay attention! This is important stuff."

I widen my eyes and give Tyler my exaggerated attention, and he chuckles at my expression.

"Okay, here's the bet, little freshman. If you last thirty seconds without laughing at me—and good luck with that, by the way—you'll get a twenty-dollar payday from Aaron. Plus, I'll have to pay that bastard thirty bucks. Not a good result for me. *But* if I get you to laugh, then *I'll* get thirty bucks from shit-for-brains over there, and you'll get zippo. Preferred result."

"When do I pay something?" I ask. "I don't have any skin in the game."

"You don't need skin in the game. You're Zooey Cartwright. Our reason for being. Plus, you're ridiculously cute. That's payment enough." He winks. "Okay, are you ready, giggler?"

I shake out my arms and nod.

Hanalei holds up his phone set to the stopwatch function. "Thirty seconds starts in three, two, one, *go.*"

Tyler smiles at me. "Hi there, cutie."

I force myself to keep a straight face. It's not easy to do

when Tyler's turning on his charm full-throttle. "Hello."

"I've got four words for you," Tyler says. He counts them off with his fingers. "Where are Pooh's pants?"

I press my lips together and stay strong.

Tyler leans forward and puts his muscled forearms on the table. "Knock, knock."

"Who's there?" I reply dutifully.

"Wherefore means."

I pause for a split second, trying to figure out where this joke is headed. "Wherefore means *who*?"

"No, Zooey Cartwright! Wherefore means *why*. How many times do I have to explain that to you?" He makes a face of complete exasperation that pulls an involuntary giggle from my throat. *Damn it!* It was just a little giggle, but it was unmistakable.

Immediately, everyone at the table explodes in protest.

"Collusion!" one guy yells.

"Damn you, Zooey Cartwright!" another one scolds.

"Are you suffering from Stockholm syndrome?" Aaron asks me. "Blink twice if you need us to save you, Zooey Cartwright!"

"Why do you guys keep calling me by my full name?" I ask, giggling even more.

Everyone ignores my question. They're too wrapped up in the money changing hands to pay attention to me. While Aaron slumps forward, shaking his head, Tyler leans back in his chair with his winnings, laughing with glee.

"Why the hell did you laugh at *that*, Zooey Cartwright?" Aaron asks. "That was the stupidest joke ever."

"Oh, and cheetahs being expelled from the zoo is so fucking clever?" Tyler says.

"It was collusion," another one of the guys proclaims again. "Plain and simple."

"It wasn't *collusion*," I insist. "Tyler made me laugh fair and square, guys."

Everyone protests, yet again.

"He did," I insist. "Tyler hit me with *Shakespeare*, guys. He knows I can't resist Shakespeare."

I'm lying, of course. Shakespeare isn't what made me laugh. In truth, it wouldn't have mattered what joke Tyler told in the end, I was going to laugh, regardless. Why? Because when I'm around Tyler, I feel like I'm sucking on nitrous oxide. Because Tyler willed me to laugh, and I can't seem to resist giving him whatever he wants, no matter what it is or what's at stake. The bare truth is that I didn't laugh because Tyler Caldwell "hit me with *Shakespeare*." I laughed because Tyler Caldwell hit me with *Tyler Caldwell*.

CHAPTER TWENTY-TWO

Everyone around me screams like we're in mutual, mortal pain. Jake Grayson just threw the perfect long ball... I mean the *perfect* spiraling pass for well over thirty yards...*and Aaron Heckerling let the dang ball slip right through his fingers*! Oh, the humanity! That was third down! *Damn!* As the offense jogs off the field and the punting unit jogs on, I take my seat again, groaning along with everyone else on my half of the stadium.

I've never had so much fun at a football game in my life. And I've been to lots of them with my dad back home, so that's saying a lot. I had no idea how much fun it would be to sit in the student section with my fellow Bruins, my face painted blue and gold, and cheer on *my* school. Not to mention the fact that I'm here with Clarissa and Dimitri and his friends, and they're the sweetest, funniest group, ever. Oh, and to top it all off, we're playing our cross-town rivals, the Trojans of USC—Boo!—and currently beating them by fourteen points—Yay! Oh, and did I mention the best part of all? I'm watching Tyler play like a god among men down on that field.

Speaking of which, Tyler makes a bone-crushing tackle on the field, and the crowd roars. I glance at the jumbo screen, hoping to catch a glimpse of Tyler's thug-face. It's the scary face he almost always makes right after making a big hit, and it never ceases to turn me on.

The view on the jumbo screen switches to an up-close shot of Tyler, but he quickly turns, and the camera catches nothing but his backside as he jogs away from his crumpled opponent. But that's okay. If I can't see Tyler's thug-face, a tight shot of his ass jogging away in his tight little pants is a lovely consolation prize.

I look at the scoreboard. There are about seven minutes to go in the third quarter. *Please, God, let us hold onto this lead and clinch the win.* So far this season, we're undefeated, and Tyler's a huge reason for that. He hasn't forced a turnover yet today, but he's been blocking passes and tackling like a man possessed. Plus, in the second quarter, he brazenly stripped the ball right out of a Trojan's hands, a maneuver that made Tyler look like a Rottweiler and the other guy look like a Chihuahua. I've got to think if any NFL teams are watching today to gather intel before the draft in the spring, Tyler's strip of that ball alone was enough to move him up several spaces on everyone's list of top prospects.

Of course, I'm thrilled Tyler's having yet another stellar game, any way he can get one, but I'd be lying if I didn't admit I'm hoping he'll grab an interception today. First off, I know that's the stat the NFL boys love to see from a guy in Tyler's position, and I want him to have every possible chance to make his top ten dreams come true. Second, I also want to see Tyler make an interception simply because I'm a card-carrying Bruin now. And that means I want our boys in blue and gold to not only kick those Trojan boys' asses today, but do it in a fashion that makes every student clad in cardinal and gold on the opposite side of this huge stadium go back to their sparkling campus across town with their designer tails between their waxed and spray-tanned legs and sob relentlessly into their high-thread-count pillow cases all night long. But, third, despite all that, the biggest reason I want Tyler to get an interception today is that when I texted him this morning to wish him luck in the game, he replied:

> *If I get an interception today, watch me close. I'll send you a secret signal, eager beaver.*

On the field, Jake counts off hard from the line. The ball is snapped. Jake hands off to his running back and, immediately, the guy gets stuffed hard at the line like he ran into a brick wall. Everyone wearing blue and gold groans in vicarious pain while the trust-fund babies on the other side of the stadium cheer wildly.

"You girls want some popcorn?" Dimitri asks, drawing my attention away from the action on the field.

"Thanks," Clarissa chirps, taking a handful of popcorn from Dimitri's bag.

I shake my head. "No, thanks. Too nervous to eat."

"Nervous?" Dimitri says. "Look at the scoreboard."

"It ain't over 'til it's over, son," I mutter. "That's why they play the game."

"True."

"I'm mostly nervous for Tyler," I admit. "He says every single game is critical for him. His goal is to go top ten in the draft."

"Wow, that's a tall order for a free safety," Dimitri says. "But, hey, if anyone can do it, it's Tyler. He's definitely having the season of a lifetime."

I return my attention to the field just in time to see Jake connect with his tight end for a first down. Everyone on our side of the stadium cheers.

"So how are things going between you and Tyler?" Dimitri asks. "I saw you two walking through South Campus the other day holding hands. You looked good together. Like Beauty and the...Beauty."

Clarissa giggles.

"Things are good," I say. "We're not officially dating. We're just, you know..." I press my lips together. We're just...*what*? Two junkies who are totally and completely addicted to each other? Because, truthfully, that's how it feels—like neither of us can ever get enough. It's enthralling and terrifying, all at once. If I feel this addicted now, I can't imagine how I'm going to feel three weeks from now when Tyler and I are supposedly going to flip some magical switch and become nothing but friends.

A collective gasp erupts in the stands, abruptly drawing my attention to the field. I gasp, too. A long pass from Jake to Aaron is spiraling through the air. Aaron is open. Running at full speed. Aaron extends his arms as he runs, and the ball lands smack into his hands midstride. The place erupts. Aaron evades a tackle. And keeps right on running. *Touchdown.*

The place goes nuts. The extra point is good. The kick-off is uneventful. And now the defense, including Tyler, is jogging onto the field. Nerves grip my stomach. *Come on, Tyler.*

I watch Tyler take his position in the backfield. He

shouts something at his teammates. Points. Shouts again. He's in command. He barks something urgently at one of his teammates in particular. The guy must be out of position. Either that or Tyler's read something in the Trojans' formation, and he's letting the guy know what he sees. *God, he's so dang good at this game.*

The ball is snapped. The quarterback for the University of Spoiled Children drops back and lets loose a beautiful spiral headed for his star receiver. And Tyler's right there. He leaps up and grabs the ball, making the entire stadium explode. He returns the interception for about twelve yards before he's taken down and, again, every Bruin in the stadium goes ballistic.

I scrutinize Tyler closely. He told me to watch him for a shout-out if he got an interception, and I can't wait to see what he'll do. But Tyler gets off the ground and calmly jogs toward the sideline, cradling his precious contraband in his bent arm. I hold my breath and wait. But, nope, he heads off the field with his entire defensive unit, without displaying even the slightest hint of excitement about his spectacular grab.

"Talk about acting like you've been there before!" Clarissa shouts to Dimitri over the crowd.

"He doesn't want to get flagged for excessive celebration," Dimitri explains, and the minute he says it, I realize he's absolutely right. *Of course.* I know about that stupid rule against celebrating—so why'd I think he'd do something outwardly detectable for me after an interception? Clearly, he just meant he'd send me a little *telepathic* shout-out if he snagged a pass. I sit back down, feeling stupid for my high expectations.

"He can't celebrate at least a little bit?" Clarissa asks, taking her seat next to me.

"Nope," Dimitri says. "He can't do the slightest thing after the play, or he'll get dinged and the play will be negated."

As our offense heads onto the field to take over, I find Tyler on the sideline. He's seated on a bench behind the coaches and players standing along the sideline. He's getting high-fives and helmet slaps from his teammates. A cameraman for the jumbo screen makes his way over to the bench where Tyler's sitting and, suddenly, his gorgeous face fills the massive screen.

And then it happens.

My secret signal.

Tyler looks straight into the camera, brings the football up to his face mask, and moves it back and forth lengthwise across his face several times. And then, following that bit of awesomeness, Tyler lowers the ball, sticks out his tongue, and makes the exact face I'd imagine a cannibal would make right after eating another guy's face off.

Clarissa laughs. "What the hell was that? Was Tyler eating corn on the cob?"

One of Dimitri's friends posits another theory. "Maybe the ball was the heart of the dude Tyler just picked off. Tyler's saying he's a fucking cannibal, man."

I don't say a word. Of course, I know they're both wrong. Obviously, that first thing was Tyler pretending to be a beaver gnawing on a log. And that maniacal tongue-face he flashed after that? That was yet another coded message to me. To my crotch, specifically. Tyler just secretly told me he's going to eat—and *savor*—his eager beaver's beaver tonight. There might be a prohibition against "excessive celebrations" on the football field, but clearly, Tyler and I are going to have our own private "excessive celebration" of his triumph tonight.

CHAPTER TWENTY–THREE

The song blaring in Tyler's bedroom is yet another from his playlist of all-time favorites: "Enter Sandman" by Metallica. And, lucky me, I'm listening to this hard-hitting, nasty song while being bent over Tyler's bed and getting pounded from behind.

Tyler leans over to my ear. His breath is hot. One hand is on my breast. His other on my clit. "I'm gonna spank your ass in three seconds unless you tell me no."

What was that now? I open my mouth to reply and close it again. *Why did Tyler ask for a no this time, rather than an explicit yes?* But before I can engage in further analysis of that puzzle, Tyler's hand leaves my breast, and I feel a stinging sensation on my right ass cheek. Well, I'll be damned. That turned me on.

"Yes?" he growls.

"*Yes.*"

Tyler continues pounding me for a bit more, and then he spanks me again...and...I...come so hard, my legs collapse underneath me. I crumple onto the bed, growling with my pleasure.

In a flash, Tyler pulls out of me, grabs the purple dildo that's been ominously sitting on the edge of the bed this whole time, and slides that sucker inside me. Without further ado, he turns it on, bends down behind me, parts my ass cheeks, and proceeds to tongue my asshole.

Almost instantly, my back-door muscles begin spasming like crazy. "Tyler," I grit out, just before my body comes like a freight train, even harder than the last time. "Oh, my God."

I hear a splooging sound, like something being squeezed out of a bottle, and then the sensation of Tyler's slick fingers sliding up and down my ass crack.

Oh, jeez. I suddenly understand what Tyler's about to do. "I'm scared," I blurt.

"Relax," Tyler whispers, his breathing labored.

I can't relax. I can't breathe. My chest is tight. "*I'm scared.*"

"I'll go slow," he whispers. "The minute you say no, it's over. No coaxing. No persuading. One 'no' and I'm immediately out. You trust me?"

I take a deep breath. "Yes."

"Tell me you trust me."

"I trust you."

"This is going to feel amazing. You'll see."

I take another deep breath.

"Yes?" he whispers.

"Yes."

He increases the speed of the vibrator inside me, sending its head knocking feverishly against my G-spot and the little silicone "rabbit" at its base swirling frenetically across my clit.

I moan. I'm shaking. Short of breath.

"Relax," he coos. He slides his finger inside my ass, past the thick ring of muscles guarding its entrance, and... Wait.

That's not Tyler's finger.

I yelp. And kind of squeak. "So big," I breathe, clutching the bedspread.

"Breathe," Tyler says into my ear. "Take a deep breath and exhale."

I do as I'm told, and he slides himself farther inside me.

"Yes?" he grits out.

"Yes," I choke out.

One more deep breath and Tyler's all the way inside me. He begins moving slowly. Holy motherfucking shit! I've got a vibrating dildo up my cooch and a giant cock up my ass? Who am I? And why does this feel so good? I make a garbled sound and tighten my grip on the bed covering. I'm hanging on for dear life.

"Oh, Jesus," Tyler gasps behind me, his voice strained. "Thank you, Jesus. You okay, baby?"

I open my mouth to reply, but a tsunami of white-hot ecstasy shoots through me, and then an orgasm like nothing I've felt before racks me—an orgasm so devastating to my system, it causes tears to spontaneously squirt out of my eyes.

I crumple, but Tyler's got me. He holds me up even as his dick ripples inside me with what feels to me like a huge orgasm for him.

Finally, we collapse onto the bed together, both of us gasping for air.

I pull the vibrating dildo out of me. Turn it off and toss it onto the bed. "Holy fuck," I say.

"Thank you, God," he whispers. He gulps at the air for a moment. "Thank you, Zooey Cartwright."

We rearrange ourselves until we're both lying on our sides, facing each other, our chests heaving. "You seemed to enjoy doing that just a little bit," I say, smiling.

"Holy shit. That was my first time. Amazing."

My eyes widen. "Seriously?"

He nods. "You de-virginized me, Zooey Cartwright."

I smile broadly. "Does that mean I'm a lifelong memory now?"

Tyler strokes my hair for a moment, looking deep in thought. He gently stretches a coiled strand of my hair taut, releases it, and watches it go *boing*. "You already were."

CHAPTER TWENTY-FOUR

It's Sunday afternoon. And for the third week in a row, I'm hanging out with Tyler at his place following a postgame sleepover. I glance up from the paper I'm editing on my laptop and peek at Tyler across the room. His T-shirt on this particular day reads Greatness. He's staring at his economics textbook and mouthing the words to the current song from his "all-time favorites" playlist, "Flagpole Sitta" by Harvey Danger. I watch him for a moment, chuckling to myself about the quirky lyrics of the song and how adorable Tyler is singing along to it. He's so sweet and funny. And *gentle.* It blows my mind he's the same guy who hurls himself at opponents like a missile on Saturdays.

"Can I ask you something?" I ask.

Tyler looks up from his book.

"How do you get yourself psyched up to be such a savage beast on the field? You're always such a sweetheart off it."

Tyler makes a face like I've said something patently stupid. "I'm not *always* a sweetheart off the field. I'm a sweetheart around *you* because you've cast some sort of Zooey Cartwright spell on me." He smiles. "But to answer your underlying question, I don't know how I turn into that madman you see on the playing field. I guess football unleashes something primal inside me. Or, actually, maybe it's the other way around. Maybe I'm innately a madman and football helps me keep myself in check the rest of the week? It definitely helps me release all my pent-up rage, that's for sure."

Fascinating. I would have expected Tyler to say football helps him release his *stress*. But his pent-up *rage*? That's a mighty strong choice of words, especially for a person I've come to regard as incredibly easygoing. "What's the source of your pent-up rage?" I ask, closing my laptop.

Tyler's features noticeably tighten. "Oh, just life's assorted fiascos and catastrophes. Nothing specific." He smiles and looks down at his book again, his body language stiff.

He's not telling me something. Obviously. Out of nowhere, something Tyler once said to me pops into my head. *My dad and sister always text me before games.* At the time, I assumed his mom wasn't included in that statement for an innocuous reason. Like, maybe she simply prefers calling her son on game days. But suddenly I'm wondering if maybe there's a different explanation for his mother's absence from that pregame ritual—like maybe his mother is absent from his life for some reason? Is he estranged from her? Did she abandon him?

I'm still turning the idea over in my head when the playlist blaring through the room switches to "Careless Whisper" by George Michael...and the song instantly transforms Tyler. Immediately, he's no longer stiff and brooding. He's light and bright. "Best song ever," Tyler declares. He begins serenading me with gusto, apparently not the least bit concerned he can't carry a tune. Oh, my God. He's absolutely adorable. "Sing with me, Zooey!" Tyler commands when the chorus arrives.

I sing as best I can, although I don't know the words nearly as well as Tyler does.

In the middle of the song, when a sax solo begins, Tyler pulls me off the bed and twirls me around the small room. He dips me. Kisses me. Literally sweeps me off my feet. And then he serenades me again in the final chorus like his heart is breaking every bit as much as George's. Finally, when the song ends, we return to Tyler's bed, laughing.

"It's official," I say. "You're the weirdo, not me."

"I told you I sing that song better than George."

"That's honestly what you think?"

"Not just me. It's what everyone says when I sing it. They say I put George to shame."

"And you wonder if the halo effect is real?"

He laughs. "You're implying I'm not genuinely brilliant at something?"

"I would never imply such blasphemy about the great Tyler Caldwell. I'm saying it outright. You suck." I beam a huge smile at him. "But you're wonderful, too. I absolutely love hearing you sing, Tyler."

He chuckles. "You've got a fantastic voice, by the way. Wow."

"That? Oh, gosh." I swat at the air. "I was just playing around. That's not how I actually *sing.*"

"Really? I thought it was damned good. Not nearly as good as *my* singing, of course. But really good."

I roll my eyes.

"No? Okay, then show me how you really do it. Sing for real."

I shake my head.

"Yes."

"No."

"Please?"

"No."

"*Pretty please.*"

"Nope."

He scowls. "Why not?"

"Too shy."

Now he looks astonished. "But you're a theater major. You want to sing on Broadway one day."

"I'm not shy about singing for an actual *audience*. I'm just shy to sing for *you*. Here in your room. Just the two of us."

Tyler looks at me quizzically.

"Onstage, there are blinding lights," I explain. "I can't see the faces. I get lost in the song. But here, when I'm just little ol' me, being asked to sing for big ol' you, it's terrifying."

Tyler takes my hand and flashes me what I'm sure he thinks is his most charming smile. "Pretty please with a cherry on top sing for me, Zooey Cartwright?"

I shake my head.

Tyler drops my hands like a hot potato. "Damn. With every other girl in the world, that would have worked like a charm. No one can resist my 'pretty please with a cherry on top' eyes."

I shrug. "Until now."

"Well, shit," Tyler says. "Can I at least watch a video of you singing for real? There's got to be something on YouTube from one of your high school musicals or whatever."

"Yeah, sure. My performance when I won this regional showcase is on YouTube. It's what got me my biggest scholarship."

"You *won*? Out of how many people?"

"To start with? Thousands. By the bitter end, maybe forty?"

"Holy shit."

"I've won lots of singing competitions. For a year, I competed in everything I could find that had scholarship money as the prize. The scholarships I won are going to pay for my first three years of expenses. After that, I'll have to work and take out loans, but it shouldn't be too bad."

"How did I not know this about you? You're a badass singer?"

I shrug.

"You've been holding out on me, Cartwright. Wow." He motions to his computer. "Well, cue that showcase up, dude. I want to see it."

I grab Tyler's laptop and navigate to YouTube. "The song I performed at that big showcase was 'Defying Gravity' from *Wicked*. It's my favorite. If ever I get to perform in *Wicked*, that'll be my version of playing in the Super Bowl. And I don't even need to be Elphaba. Even if I'm just in the chorus, whether on Broadway or just touring, I'll feel like I've arrived. But if I *do* get to be Elphaba one day, especially on Broadway, oh my freaking God, that'll be like winning ten Super Bowls and being named MVP in all of them."

"I've never heard of *Wicked*."

"Never heard of *Wicked*? What? First Babar, then Josie

and the Pussycats, and now *this*? Tyler Caldwell!"

He chuckles. "What's it about?"

"It's a prequel to *The Wizard of Oz*. It's about how this green-skinned girl named Elphaba grows up to become the Wicked Witch of the West. She wasn't wicked to start with—in fact, she was genuinely kind-hearted and good. She was just always misunderstood and ostracized because of her green skin. I guess you could say poor Elphaba experienced the opposite of the halo effect, thanks to her skin color."

"Wow. It sounds cool."

"Oh, God, it is, Tyler. I love it so, so much." I find the link to the showcase video and cue it up. "When my grandparents took me to New York for the first time at age ten, they took me to see *Wicked* on Broadway, and I swear to God in that moment, I knew exactly..." Something in the way Tyler's looking at me makes me trail off. "Why are you... What?"

Tyler smiles. "You're totally lit up right now, Zooey. Like a Christmas tree. This is by far the sexiest you've ever looked to me. And that's saying a lot."

I blush.

"But go on. I'm listening. I'm hard as a rock, but I'm listening."

My heart is racing. "I was just saying that, um... What was I saying? Oh, yeah. When I saw *Wicked* for the first time, I realized the most important thing about me."

"What's that?"

"I'm destined to be a performer. It's literally the only thing I want to do with my life. And that I'm supposed to wind up on Broadway one day. That I can't stop working toward that goal until I achieve it." My jaw tightens. "Getting onto Broadway is my life's purpose. And the pinnacle of that destiny will be me playing Elphaba on Broadway." I clutch my heart. It's racing. "If I reach that peak, I'll know I've lived the best life humanly possible."

Tyler smiles.

"But I'm sure you can understand. You must dream of playing in the Super Bowl."

"All the time. Among other things."

"When did you first realize football is your life's purpose?" I ask.

"Oh, football isn't my life's purpose," he says, shocking me. "It's the vehicle for me to reach my higher destiny, for sure, but it's not my life's purpose. The same way boxing wasn't Muhammad Ali's life's purpose."

"What was his life's purpose?"

"Ali was put on this earth to inspire greatness in others through displaying his own greatness. His true purpose was to use his charisma and star power to change people's hearts and minds and make the world a better place. His purpose transcended boxing."

My lips part in surprise.

"I've got a God-given gift for playing football," Tyler says. "I know that. But my true purpose is figuring out how to harness that power to make an impact beyond football. Not just for my own personal wealth and success, which, of course, is part of what motivates me, but I also genuinely want to make the world a better place."

Okay. That's it. I'm totally screwed. I just fell head over

heels in love with Tyler Caldwell. And not because of any freaking halo effect, either. But because he's the most beautiful human being I've ever met, both inside and out.

For a long moment, I'm too mesmerized to speak. Or think. Or *breathe*. But, finally, I pull myself together and say, "You know, Tyler, you really should try dreaming a bit bigger sometimes. You never know what could happen if you just put your mind to it."

We both burst out laughing.

"Okay, enough trying to distract me," Tyler says. He indicates his laptop. "Let's see that video."

"Nope," I say. I pull the laptop away from his greedy fingertips as he reaches for it.

"Aw, come on, Zooey!"

"Hang on." I navigate to a new video—a karaoke track for "Defying Gravity." "I've changed my mind." I look up at him and smile. "I've decided to sing it for you live."

CHAPTER TWENTY-FIVE

After the last soaring note of "Defying Gravity" leaves my lips, I close my mouth and lock eyes with Tyler. He's sitting on the edge of his bed, his eyes glistening and his chest rising and falling sharply. He looks the same way he did recently after I'd given him a particularly "artistic" blow job.

Tyler stands. "That was incredible, Zooey." He moves to me and peels off my shirt. And then his. "I'm so hard right now." He's got my shorts off. "When you hit that high note, I got an instant boner." We're both naked now. He pulls me onto the bed. In a flash, his warm skin is covering mine. His uncovered hard-on is jutting against my wet entrance. He slides his tip against my tingling clit, making it ache. "You're God's gift to the world," he murmurs, kissing me. "I can't believe you're all mine."

Goose bumps erupt all over my body. *I'm all his?* "Tyler," I whisper. But that's all I can manage.

He reaches down and massages my tip.

And I'm instantly gone.

"I'm coming," I choke out.

"You're so sexy." He raises my arms above my head, pins my wrists together with one of his large hands, and kisses me as I climax. "I can't wait to feel greatness surrounding my cock.

But first, I want to *taste* it."

As Tyler's hungry lips make their way down to my belly toward the sensitive folds between my legs, I let out a long, low moan, anticipating his mouth's ultimate landing spot.

"You defy gravity, Zooey," he says softly from between my legs. His warm, wet tongue finds my clit, making me groan. "Your *pussy* defies gravity, baby."

Um. Logically, I don't know what that last comment means exactly, but logic has no place here. The way he said it turned me on. I buck and gyrate and push myself into Tyler's voracious mouth, aching for another climax that's already brewing inside me. He slides his fingers inside my wetness and his thumb up my ass while continuing to lick me...and... oh, God, *yes*...in short order, my body once again racks with shockwaves of pleasure.

"I want you," I breathe. I feel desperate for him. "Fuck me, Tyler."

Tyler grabs a condom from his drawer and gets himself covered in record speed. When he returns to me, he slides a pillow underneath the small of my back, pushes my thighs to my chest, folds me like a beach chair, and slides his full length into me with breathtaking ease. "Zooey," he whispers. "You're fucking amazing."

I hitch my legs up around Tyler's ribcage as he thrusts into me. Dig my fingernails into his forearms as he holds my thighs in place. "Deeper," I whisper. "As deep as you can go. Oh, God, yes. Deeper than you've ever gone."

After a few minutes of enduring Tyler's powerful thrusting, my body releases with an orgasm so intense, tears well in my eyes. Or, heck, I don't know. Maybe water is spouting from my tear ducts simply because I sang my favorite song to Tyler—the one that honestly expresses the most important thing there is to know about my soul—and it made him hard for me.

On the heels of my orgasm, Tyler impales me, snaps his hips forward, lets out a loud growl, and collapses on top of me. Several more jerks and shudders on top of me and his body finally goes completely quiet.

For a long moment, we lie in a crumpled, intertwined heap, gasping for air, until Tyler lifts his head and opens his mouth like he's going to say something. But when he sees the tears streaking my cheeks, his brow instantly knits with concern. "Did I hurt you?"

I shake my head.

"Then what's that clear liquid coming out of those pretty blue things in your face?"

I wipe my cheeks. Try to smile. *Oh, God, I want to tell him the truth.* That I'm crying because I just realized I feel closer to him than I've felt to anyone in my life. And that I can't bear the idea of us being nothing more than friends mere weeks from now. But I'm quite certain a reply like that would break every rule of our arrangement and possibly spur him into breaking things off with me prematurely. And so, I take a deep breath and say, "Sometimes, when a girl's body feels really, really good, liquid spontaneously squirts out her peep holes."

Tyler laughs and pushes a lock of hair out of my eyes. "Promise me something, Zooey Cartwright."

I hold my breath.

"Promise me you'll never give up on chasing your big

dreams."

Oh, well that's an easy one. "I promise."

"And promise you'll start dreaming even bigger than being Alfalfa on Broadway."

"*Elphaba.*"

"Whatever. You're filled with greatness, baby. That means you need to start dreaming way bigger than being Elphaba, sweetheart. Bigger than you think you have a right to dream. Don't tamp down your greatness to fit in or make people around you feel better about their own absence of greatness. Greatness like yours is rare in this world. A precious gift." His eyes are on fire. "It's not arrogance to think you can change the world, Zooey. When you have greatness inside you, it's your *duty* to believe that."

He's rendered me speechless. I nod, but only because I don't know what else to do.

Tyler strokes my cheek for a moment, apparently deep in thought. And then he smiles at me, gently pulls on a lock of my curly hair, and watches it bounce and re-coil when he releases it. "Promise me you won't rest until the entire world has heard that incredible voice of yours, Zooey. Anything short of that, God's going to be pissed he picked *you* of all his children to gift the voice of an angel."

CHAPTER TWENTY-SIX

It's a Tuesday night at Tyler's house. As I walked through the front door several hours ago, I immediately insisted Tyler and I rehearse our scene from *Romeo and Juliet* right away, before we let ourselves get hopelessly distracted the way we always do.

"Absolutely," Tyler agreed. "Just let me take a quick shower. I just got home. I'm all sweaty."

"Sure. But right after that, okay?"

"You bet."

So, of course, I joined Tyler in the shower. That was a no-brainer. And we wound up having some yummy sex that took way longer than either of us had planned. But who could blame us? The hot water was raining down on us, making our skin all hot and pink and slippery and delicious. So who could possibly rush anything under circumstances like that? And then, immediately after our shower, Tyler and I didn't get to rehearsing our scene right away, either, but that was only because we were both feeling extremely relaxed and happy from our sexy shower, and Tyler was feeling exhausted from his long day of practice and workouts and classes. Under the circumstances, it only seemed fair to let the poor guy unwind for a bit by watching an episode of *The Office*.

"Just one episode, Tyler," I warned sternly. "And then it's time for *Romeo and Juliet*, whether you like it or not."

"Absolutely."

With our one-episode pact firmly agreed upon, we snuggled up together in Tyler's bed and turned on Netflix and happily joined our virtual best friends at the fictional paper company, Dunder Mifflin, for some hijinks. Five episodes later, when Hanalei shouted up the stairs to ask if we wanted to join the rest of the guys for fish tacos in the Village, we called back "*Si, señor!*" But that was a no-brainer, too. I mean, come on, it's Taco Tuesday.

Finally, when Tyler and I returned to the house after tacos with the guys—during which we played yet another round of Make Zooey Cartwright Laugh, this time with no money at stake, thank God—we marched straight up to Tyler's room, vowing to practice our Shakespeare scene immediately. But we didn't manage it quite yet. It wasn't our fault, though. What sane person wouldn't get a little distracted after putting on those sparkling masks? They're sexy as hell. So, yeah, we wound up having enthusiastic sex, yet again, this time against Tyler's bedroom wall. Right against the poster of that football player I don't recognize in the Broncos uniform. Note to self: Ask Tyler who that Bronco is.

After that, I made Tyler watch Cartoon Network for a bit, but only because I'd made yet another cartoon-related joke that Tyler didn't get—this time referencing *Steven Universe*. I mean, come on! He'd never even heard of it! So, of course, we watched an episode, and Tyler laughed uproariously several times.

And now, *finally*, Tyler and I are sitting on the edge of his bed, rehearsing our scene from *Romeo and Juliet* while wearing nothing but our underwear and masquerade masks. All in all, a damned fine Tuesday night, I must say, even if we're not going to win any awards for academic productivity.

"O, then, dear saint, let lips do what hands do," Tyler says, his palm pressed against mine. He scowls. "Shoot. What's my line?" He snaps his fingers like a thespian summoning a lowly stagehand. "Line!"

I giggle. "They pray, grant thou, lest faith turn to despair."

"Shit. I'm never going to be able to memorize this damned scene."

"Yes, you are. If we practice the scene enough times, you'll memorize it without even trying. That's why I keep nagging at you to rehearse."

"Can't I just read from the book when we perform it for our class?"

I'm aghast. "Blasphemy! Oh, my God, Tyler. My heart." I clutch my chest. "If you're on-book during the performance, you won't be able to completely immerse yourself in Romeo's *emotional life.*"

Tyler rolls his eyes behind his mask. "That was literally the most theater-major thing you've ever said."

I ignore his jab. "This scene is about Romeo seeing Juliet for the first time and feeling like he's been struck by a thunderbolt. He sees her, and he's instantly positive she's his *destiny.* You won't be able to convey Romeo's heart-stopping, all-encompassing, written-in-the-stars attraction to Juliet if you're staring at the pages of your textbook."

Tyler sighs. "It'd be a whole lot easier if those two knuckleheads would just speak plain English."

I giggle. "And what would those two knuckleheads say if they did?"

"They wouldn't say 'lest faith turn to despair,' that's for fucking sure."

Oh my God, he's so cute when he's annoyed. "What would Romeo say in plain English? We might as well start fleshing out the companion contemporary scene we're supposed to write. We're way behind on that."

Tyler considers his reply. "Well, this scene is about Romeo seeing Juliet at a party and feeling like she's his idea of the perfect girl, right?"

"That's a great way to explain it. Yes."

"Well, then, that's easy. Romeo would say to Juliet whatever I said to you when I first saw you at the party."

My heart stops. *Oh, my God.*

"Do you remember what I said to you when I first approached you?" Tyler asks breezily, apparently unaware of the heart-stopping dots he's just connected. "I could barely think when I first saw you. You were so gorgeous, you fried my brain. Plus, I was drunk that night, which wasn't typical for me."

My heart is racing. "Yeah, um, I remember exactly what we both said. You were like, 'Hey, I'm Tyler Caldwell.' And then I said something like 'Gah-buh-dah-boo-gah.' And then you said, 'I don't go for freshmen because they're batshit crazy.' And I said something like, 'That's dumb.' And then you said, 'Rules were made to be broken.'" I laugh. "We weren't the second coming of Romeo and Juliet, to be honest."

Tyler chuckles. "Okay, then we should make our modern-day Romeo say what I was *thinking* when I saw you, not what I actually said. That ought to give our modern-day Juliet something more interesting to work with."

The hairs on my arms stand up. "What were you thinking when you saw me?"

Tyler scoots closer to me on the edge of the bed. He grabs my hand. "Hey there. I saw you across the crowded kitchen and couldn't believe my eyes. You're the most gorgeous girl I've ever seen in my life. *My idea of perfect.* The minute I saw you, every other girl at this party faded away. Every other girl in the world, as a matter of fact. Suddenly, it was just you and me and my very hard cock." He smiles and leans toward me, sending my heart fluttering. "Beautiful girl, I want to kiss you so fucking bad—more than I want to draw my next breath."

My cheeks feel hot. I nod and pucker, and he leans in and kisses me.

And that's it. I lose my mind. I throw my arms around Tyler's neck and slide onto his lap and straddle him and attack him—and not ten seconds later, Tyler's Shakespeare textbook has landed with a thud onto the floor, our masks and underwear are off and thrown willy-nilly across the room, and our *Romeo and Juliet* rehearsal is officially done for the night.

CHAPTER TWENTY-SEVEN

It's Wednesday night, and I'm at Tyler's house. Once again, we're practicing our Shakespearean scene in his bedroom.

"Then move not, while my prayer's effect I take," Tyler says, his blue eyes glinting behind his mask. "This is where I kiss you, right?"

I nod.

Tyler pulls me close and lays a sexy kiss on my lips. And then he whispers, without needing to glance at the book sitting next to him on the bed, "Thus from my lips, by thine, my sin is purged."

"Then have my lips the sin that they have took," I reply.

"Sin from thy lips?" Tyler replies. "O trespass sweetly urged! Give me my sin again."

He kisses me again, only this time like he's going to fuck the living hell out of me.

"Oh, my God. That was amazing, Tyler!" I'm giddy with excitement. "You were amazing! My only note is that you can't kiss me quite that passionately when we perform it for the class. But, otherwise, it was absolutely perfect."

"Why can't I kiss you that passionately? Romeo and Juliet are totally hot for each other. You said Romeo feels like he was struck by a thunderbolt."

"Yeah, but they just met."

"So what? Five minutes after I met you, we were swallowing each other's faces and dry-humping each other on a dance floor."

"Things were different back then. The slightest kiss was a huge thing."

"Oh, come on. You think Romeo would have been any less hot for Juliet than I was for you out of the gate, just because it was the sixteenth century? For fuck's sake, the dude kills himself over her at the end. That's some next-level passion, son. I say we let the poor guy mack down on his bae the same way I macked down on you."

"No, we need to do a stage kiss. Like this." I give him a prim, little peck.

Tyler shakes his head. "Juliet's not his *sister*. When Romeo sees her, she ignites a forest fire in the depths of his *soul*. He instantly knows she's the answer to a prayer he didn't even know he had. Yes, as it turns out at the end, they're star-crossed lovers and totally doomed, but Romeo doesn't know that when he first lays eyes on her. All he knows is he wants that girl more than he wants to breathe. More than he ever thought possible. He feels like he's going to die if he doesn't get a taste of her perfect lips. And that means Romeo needs to kiss Juliet exactly the way I kissed you at the party."

Um... Did Tyler just say what I think he said? I clutch my heart, feeling like it just exploded all over the Muhammad Ali poster on the nearby wall. But Tyler seems oblivious to what he's just implied. Indeed, he forges right ahead, apparently determined to convince me he's in the right about the appropriate level of heat for our theatrical kiss.

"Zooey, you're the one who always says great acting isn't *pretending*—that it's telling the *truth*. So let's tell the truth about how a young, horny, hopeless romantic would kiss his dream girl when given the chance. I guarantee you, whether the story takes place today or five hundred years ago, that dude's going to kiss the hell out of that girl, the same way I kissed you our first night on the dance floor."

I'm blown away. Utterly incapable of forming words.

"Good. So it's settled then," Tyler declares, apparently misinterpreting my stunned silence as agreement.

I quickly gather myself. "No, Tyler. No matter how passionately Romeo might have felt about Juliet, you still can't kiss me with that much heat in front of our class. No way."

"Why not? They're all adults. They can handle it."

I shake my head. "If you kiss me with that much passion, everyone will know we've been having sex."

"We have. No shame in that."

"No shame for *you*. But everyone knows your reputation, Tyler. They'll assume I'm just another one of your many conquests, and I don't want people thinking that about me. It's embarrassing."

"Who cares what anyone else thinks about us? As long as we both know you're not some 'conquest' of mine, that's all that matters."

My heart lurches into my throat. "I'm not a conquest?"

Tyler scoffs. "Don't be ridiculous, Zooey. Of course, not."

I shouldn't do it. I really shouldn't. But I can't help myself. "What am I, then, if you had to put a word to it?"

Tyler takes off his masquerade mask, so I do the same.

"You're my beaver. My adorable, weird, sexy, talented, funny, sexpot of an eager beaver."

I make a face that says, *Not what I was hoping for.*

Tyler exhales. "Aw, Zooey." He rubs his forehead. "I don't like labels. We are what we are. It is what it is. We're just doing our thing, feeling what we feel. There's no need to call it anything in particular. A label won't change anything."

I remain stone-faced. *A label will change everything,* I think. But I don't say it.

"Okay, here's what I know," Tyler says. He counts off on his fingers. "One, I'm having a blast with you—in and out of bed. Two, since I met you, I've been playing the best football of my life." He shrugs. "So I'm just trying not to think too much about what it all means, or I'm afraid I'll fuck everything up. It's so damned awesome, why fuck it up?" He looks at me with pleading eyes. "Okay?"

I scoot closer to him, put my palms onto his cheeks, and kiss him. "Okay."

"You're my eager little beaver," he whispers softly into my mouth. "That's all I know. My dorky, weird Zooey Cartwright who's going to be a star one day. And that's all I need to know."

CHAPTER TWENTY-EIGHT

The halo effect is real, folks. At least, according to the four social psychology experiments Tyler and Dimitri conducted today, with an assist by Clarissa and me.

In our first experiment of the day, Dimitri and Tyler stood on opposite street corners in downtown LA, and while Clarissa and I observed them, they asked passersby to sign a petition for "equality." What kind of equality? On behalf of whom and where would the petition be submitted? The boys didn't specify. Instead, the guys identified their organization simply as "People for the Equality of People." If asked any questions, we gave them a few vague, pre-scripted comments they were allowed to state in nothing but a flat, polite tone. No flirting. No turning on the charm. "And absolutely no panty-melting smiles, *Tyler Caldwell*!" I commanded right before we got started.

And guess what happened? Tyler wound up getting thirty-three signatures to Dimitri's four. *Four!* Clarissa and I couldn't believe it. Of course, we didn't tell the guys the shocking tallies at the time because we didn't want to influence their confidence levels during future experiments throughout the day. But we girls knew right then and there poor Dimitri was in for a very long and humbling day.

For our second experiment, we repeated the first one to the letter, *except* this time the guys were allowed to be as gregarious and charming as possible. The result? Tyler got a whopping eighty-six signatures, while Dimitri got seventeen.

"I slayed it that time," Dimitri declared confidently when our group reconvened briefly after our second experiment. "In fact, I wouldn't be surprised if I beat Tyler's extremely muscular ass that time."

Yet again, Clarissa and I didn't reveal the tallies onsite. But we exchanged a look that said, "Poor Dimitri."

For our third experiment, Tyler and Dimitri held up signs offering free hugs to any and all passersby...and, once again, Tyler gave away exponentially more hugs than Dimitri.

At that point, the four of us took a break to eat lunch at a nearby deli, during which we plotted our then-upcoming fourth and final experiment of the day: Tyler and Dimitri soliciting a dollar donation in exchange for the telling of a clean joke, all proceeds to benefit charity.

"Tyler and I should tell the exact same jokes, word for word," Dimitri suggested during our lunch. "Same jokes, different result, we'll know it must have been the joke-teller that made the difference."

"Excellent idea, Nerd," I agreed.

And so, we promptly proceeded to compile our list of stupid jokes, one contribution from each team member.

My joke? "What did the ocean say to the beach? Nothing. It just waved."

Clarissa's contribution: "What type of bee produces milk? A boo-bee."

Tyler's joke: "What did the buffalo say to his son when he dropped him off at college? Bison."

And, finally, Dimitri's highly intellectual contribution: "What do you call a guy with a rubber toe? Roberto."

For some reason, we laughed ourselves silly the most about Dimitri's joke, probably because it seemed especially funny to hear such a ridiculously stupid joke come out of Dimitri's incredibly intelligent mouth.

"What charity should we choose?" I asked the group, chomping on my turkey sandwich. "Anyone have a particular cause you want to support?"

"Breast cancer research," Tyler said without hesitation, before anyone else could say a word.

"Great idea," Dimitri replied breezily. "People always like donating to that one."

But one glimpse at Tyler's face and I knew he hadn't suggested breast cancer research because "people" always like donating to that cause. I understood Tyler had picked it for a deeply personal reason. And that's when I remembered Tyler telling me his dad and sister always text him on game days...and not mentioning his mom. And that made me wonder if maybe fickle Fortune had gotten its grubby paws on Tyler's mom the same way it had gotten its paws on my own?

Oh, how my heart panged for my beautiful Tyler when that horrible possibility occurred to me. But, somehow, I held it together and quietly continued eating my sandwich without saying a word. Clearly, it wasn't the right time to ask Tyler about why he'd picked breast cancer research as our chosen charity. It was time for us to head back to our opposing corners in downtown LA and let the boys try to raise some money.

And so, that's what we did.

And that completed our first round of experiments. After that, we left downtown LA and reconvened our social psychology fiesta on Bruin Walk outside UCLA's student center, the one place in the world where everybody knows—and worships—Tyler Caldwell. And that's where we repeated all four experiments again, right down the line—the new location selected to help us answer the burning question, Does celebrity status demonstrably increase the power of the halo effect? We were dying to find out.

And now, here we are, sitting in the campus Starbucks after completing all four experiments on Bruin Walk.

First off, I divulge the tallies from the first three experiments in both locations and everyone looks stunned.

"Well, shit," Dimitri says. "I thought I kicked Tyler's ass at least a couple times today. Especially in the experiments when I was allowed to be charming. I thought I was kicking ass those times."

"I swear the point wasn't to make you feel like a loser, Dimitri," I say. "We were just trying to determine if the halo effect is real."

"Well, I think we can safely conclude it is." He looks at Tyler. "Promise me you'll always use your powers for good, man. Because if you're secretly a madman hell-bent on destroying the universe, we're all fucked."

Tyler laughs. "I'm as shocked as you are about these results. Especially for that one time when we weren't allowed to be charming at all. I swear I tried to have all the charisma of a potted plant that time."

"Gee, thanks for rubbing it in," Dimitri says, but he's laughing.

"You know what would be fun?" Clarissa says. "We should do all four experiments again, but next time, Dimitri should be instructed to be as charming as possible and Tyler should try to be as boring as possible the whole time. That ought to be interesting."

"Interesting?" Dimitri says. "No, it'll be soul-crushing for me. All we'll prove is that people strongly prefer a ridiculously good-looking potted plant to a nice guy with a fantastic personality."

"Well, I don't care what anyone else prefers," Clarissa says, laying her hand on Dimitri's forearm. "I personally prefer a nice guy with a fantastic personality every time."

Dimitri blushes. "Thank you." He lays a sweet little kiss on Clarissa's cheek.

I smile at Tyler. "Me, too."

Tyler shoots me a truly lovely smile, letting me know he's understood my message loud and clear.

"So what were the tallies on the joke-telling experiment in both locations?" Dimitri asks.

I peel my eyes off Tyler's smiling face and give the group the tallies. "So it was actually relatively close when we did it downtown. That suggests humor and charity might be the great equalizer for people. But when we did it again on campus where everyone worships the ground Tyler walks on, his productivity shot up by almost four hundred percent. Oh, my God, it was a bloodbath."

"Wow," Clarissa says. "So does that mean celebrity status is the halo effect on steroids?"

"Definitely," Dimitri says. "That's why so many brands and charities use celebrities to sell products and raise money. We're all lemmings."

Tyler rubs his palms together and lets out an evil laugh. "Oh, man, one day soon I'm going to conquer the world!"

We all laugh at his exuberance.

"No doubt about it," Dimitri says. "Based on today's results, Tyler's going to become the Michael Jordan of football."

"Actually, not to be an egomaniac or anything, but Jordan's only *one* of the four greatest Michaels of all time. I'm going to be the single greatest Tyler of all-time *ever*."

"The four greatest Michaels?" Dimitri asks, laughing. "Who are the other three?"

Of course, I know the answer to this question. I've seen Tyler's Four Greatest Michaels of All Time poster on his wall countless times. But I wouldn't dream of stealing Tyler's thunder.

"Jackson, Phelps, and Scott," Tyler replies.

"*Scott?*" Clarissa asks. "Who's Michael *Scott?*"

"It's Steve Carell's character on *The Office,*" Tyler says.

"Tyler's obsessed with that show," I explain. "And now he's got me obsessed, too."

"Zooey and I are on season three," Tyler says proudly.

"It's awesome. Pam and Jim are *finally* about to get together. I can *feel* it. I keep begging Tyler to let me skip ahead so I can see them get together, but he won't let me."

"Patience, eager beaver," Tyler says, grabbing my hand. He addresses Dimitri and Clarissa. "*The Office* is but one of the great pleasures of life I've shown my little freshman these past few weeks." He smiles suggestively.

"*Tyler.*" I blush crimson at his obvious sexual innuendo.

"What?" Tyler replies innocently. "The other great pleasure is fish tacos. What did you think I meant?"

Everyone laughs.

Clarissa beams a huge, knowing smile at me and pops out of her seat. "Hey, Zo. I'm going to the bathroom. Come with me."

"Sure."

And off we go.

The minute Clarissa and I are in the restroom together, she closes the door behind us and whips around, her face aglow. "Tyler's in love with you."

I gasp. "*You think?*"

"Oh, my God. It's so freaking obvious. I knew you were falling for him, and frankly, I was kind of worried about you getting your little heart broken by him. But now that I've seen the two of you together—and especially the way he looks at you—there's no doubt in my mind he's fallen for you, too."

My heart is clanging wildly. I wring my hands together, too overwhelmed to speak.

"Tyler hasn't told you how he's feeling about you?" Clarissa asks.

"He said he's enjoying hanging out with me. And that he doesn't like labels. But he hasn't addressed the million-dollar question of what's going to happen at the five-week mark. As far as I know, he's still planning on us magically turning into friends right after we turn in our two midterm projects."

Clarissa shakes her head emphatically. "That might have been what Tyler said at the beginning, but clearly, things have changed for him. He's totally smitten."

I take a deep breath, praying she's right.

"Zooey, don't leave this to chance. Just tell him how you feel."

I shake my head.

"*Yes*. If Tyler's not going to broach the subject, then you need to do it."

I shake my head again.

"*Yes*. One of you needs to get the ball rolling. Clearly, your initial 'arrangement' has morphed into something different now. Anyone can see you two are totally into each other."

"I can't, Clarissa. When Tyler and I talked about his 'syllabus' at the beginning, he was abundantly clear about what he wants. If he's feeling differently now, then he needs to be the one who says so first."

"But, Zooey. It's so obvious you're both totally and completely smitten with each other."

My heart leaps. God, I hope she's right about that. "You're just going to have trust me on this, Clarissa. I nudged him a little bit last week, and he didn't take the bait. He practically begged me to drop it. So, now, I'm just going to keep my mouth shut and enjoy the ride." I sigh. "The truth is I'm ninety-nine percent sure falling in love isn't on Tyler's syllabus. And telling him how I'm feeling—just so he can reject me and smash my heart into a million tiny pieces—most definitely isn't on mine."

CHAPTER TWENTY-NINE

"When are you going to tell me where you're taking me?" I ask excitedly.

"Patience, eager beaver. You'll see when we get there."

Tyler and I are having this conversation in Hanalei's car on a Wednesday evening. Tyler's driving. I'm giddy. And he's looking like a million bucks in a blue, tailored suit.

I fidget with the hem of my little red dress. "Aw, come on, dude. Have mercy on me. I'm dying here."

"Sucks to be you, I guess."

"Damn."

This is torture. The only thing Tyler said about tonight's surprise was that I should wear the sexiest dress in my closet. So, of course, since I don't own a single sexy dress, I raided Clarissa's closet. The dress I picked out resembles the one I wore the night Tyler and I met a month ago, actually. But tonight, with my hair wild and my makeup barely there, I don't feel like I'm disappearing into a costume the way I did that fateful night. To the contrary, tonight, I feel like I'm revealing my most authentic self.

I look out the car window, trying in vain to discern from the passing scenery where Tyler's taking me. But it's a pointless endeavor. I don't know Los Angeles at all. "Just gimme a little hint," I say in my most persuasive voice.

"Okay, okay. Here's a little hint."

I hold my breath.

"You're going to like it."

I roll my eyes. "*Lame.* I'll like anything, as long as I'm with you. Tell me more than *that.*"

Tyler laughs. "Nope."

The song on the radio ends and, by total coincidence, "Crash into Me" begins.

Tyler turns up the radio. "Ah, now that's the soundtrack of a great memory."

I open my mouth to agree when my eyes spy a neon-lit theater up the street...with a marquee that boasts, in large black lettering, *WICKED*!

I shriek at the top of my lungs. "Tyler! Oh, my God, Tyler!" I point up the street toward the theater. "Please tell me that's where you're taking me!"

Tyler laughs. "Of course it is, baby. I figured I should see what inspired my eager little beaver on her path to greatness."

An hour and a half later...

I squeeze Tyler's hand. We've finally reached the moment I've been waiting for—the moment toward the end of the first act when Elphaba begins singing "Defying Gravity." As the first notes of the song begin, I glance at Tyler for the hundredth time since the show began, dying to see his reaction, and the look on his face doesn't disappoint. He looks precisely the way I feel. *Electrified.*

Midway through the song, Elphaba's body begins physically rising off the stage. *She's literally defying gravity up there!* Up, up, up Elphaba goes, her voice soaring and rising along with her body. I squeeze Tyler's hand again, feeling like I'm going to faint from pure joy. Sharing this with Tyler is the most exciting moment of my life.

The actress onstage hits the highest note of the song from her perch in the air, and goose bumps erupt across my skin. I look at Tyler again. His eyes are glistening and wide. His mouth is shaped into a cartoon-like "O." He looks absolutely bowled over.

A tidal wave of emotion rises up inside me. Joy. Gratitude. *Love.* I squeeze Tyler's hand for the millionth time, and he turns his head and beams at me. His eyes are sparkling. His face is flushed. He kisses the top of my hand. And, suddenly, I can't stuff down my emotions any longer. I let my tears flow.

CHAPTER THIRTY

Tyler parks Hanalei's car on a remote overlook in the Hollywood Hills where we can take in the glittering lights of the City of Angels yawning before us. By chance, the song on the car radio is "Alive" by P.O.D.

"The perfect song for this perfect moment," Tyler says softly.

And that's all the conversation we're going to have, apparently. In a flash, we mutually attack each other like animals. Two minutes later, we're in the back seat, making love furiously.

"You sing that song way better than her," Tyler whispers into my ear as his body thrusts in and out of mine.

It's the same comment he made the second after Elphaba had finished singing "Defying Gravity" tonight. And the same thing he said again after the lights came up in the theater. And the same thing he said a third time when we'd first settled into Hanalei's car in the theater parking lot.

And every single time, it's been a ridiculous thing to say. Elphaba was flawless perfection on that stage tonight. Every bit as good as the one I saw on Broadway as a child. But I don't contradict Tyler this time the way I've done earlier tonight. His words are turning me on too much to do anything but sigh and revel in the enthralling sound of his voice. Indeed, each sexy word of praise and adulation he whispers into my ear in this moment is drawing me closer and closer to a delicious climax. And, God knows, I wouldn't dream of doing anything to derail that.

"Tyler," I whisper, on the bitter edge of release. "Tonight was amazing."

"You're destined for greatness, baby," he whispers, his voice strained, his body moving magically on top of me. "The sky's the limit for you, sweetheart."

I come. *Hard.* And right after I do, Tyler follows. Clearly, he'd been hanging on solely for my benefit.

After our bodies have quieted down, we pull our disheveled clothes back together and sit cuddled together in the backseat, gazing at the glittering view.

"I didn't say all that stuff about Elphaba just to say it," Tyler says after a while. "That actress was amazing tonight— she gave me chills. But you're better than her, Zooey. That's an objective fact."

"Oh, *Tyler.*" I sigh happily and lace my fingers in his. "Thank you."

"Sing me a little something," he coos. He leans forward and turns off the car radio. "I want to hear your magnificent voice while I look at this magnificent view."

To my surprise, his request doesn't cause me the slightest bit of anxiety. On the contrary, I *want* to sing for him. And so, I do. I sing him my favorite song in the world, Leonard Cohen's "Hallelujah." And when I'm done, Tyler puts his finger underneath my chin and kisses my lips with what can only be described as *reverence*.

"Where did you get that voice of yours?" he asks. "Are your parents amazing singers, too?"

My stomach clenches. "My dad has a pleasant voice. He sings on-key, unlike someone else I know." I nudge Tyler's arm and he chuckles.

"So your mom is the one who gave you your voice, then?"

My heart lurches into my mouth. I clear my throat. "Yeah, definitely. From what I've seen on videos, my mother had an absolutely glorious voice."

Tyler stiffens next to me.

Time stops.

I take a deep breath. "My mom died in a car accident when I was two."

Tyler looks down at his lap. His shoulders droop. He puts his arm around my shoulders and pulls me into him. "I'm really sorry to hear that, Zooey."

I pause to allow Tyler to say more. If my hunch about Tyler losing his mom to breast cancer is correct, now would be an obvious time for him to tell me about it. But, nope, Tyler doesn't say a word. So I continue. "It's been hard to grow up without a mother, but I sometimes think it would have been even harder if I'd been older at the time of her death—if I'd been aware of losing her." I await Tyler's reply again. But, still, he says nothing. *Huh.* Maybe I've jumped to the wrong conclusion about his mom? "Tyler, can I ask you something?" I ask cautiously. "Why did you say your father and sister text you on game days, but you didn't mention your mom?"

Tyler looks out the far window. He exhales. "Because my

mom died when I was eleven."

My heart pangs. "Breast cancer?" I ask softly.

"Yeah."

I wait for what seems like a long time. "I'm sorry, Tyler," I finally say.

"I think about her every day," Tyler says.

"Will you tell me about her?" I ask.

Tyler takes a deep breath. He clears his throat. "I don't normally talk about her. I get too choked up."

"I understand."

"But I'll tell you." He pauses. Exhales. "She was generally kind of quiet. *Unless* she was watching football. And then she was the loudest person in any room." He smiles at some memory, and moonlight glints off his beautiful eyes. "She didn't tell a lot of jokes, but she laughed at everyone else's, especially mine, even the lame ones. *Especially* the lame ones." He pauses again. "She loved music, even though she couldn't sing worth a damn, just like me. She used to roll down the windows in her car and sing along to her favorite songs at top volume, not caring if she was in key or not. My sister and I would sit in the backseat and sing along with her and laugh and laugh." He smiles, even though tears have quite obviously pooled in the bottoms of his eyes. "My favorite thing was to watch her eyes in the rearview mirror when she was singing. They were the most beautiful blue eyes. Sometimes, she'd catch me looking at her and wink at me, and I'd wink back." His voice quavers. He wipes his eyes. "Lots of times, I could feel her looking at me when I was doing nothing, like maybe sitting at the kitchen table doing homework. I'd look up and she'd just be standing there watching me with this look of pure love on her face." He sighs. "And I could physically *feel* her love for me."

I squeeze his hand. "Was she sick for a long time?"

He nods. "I was eight the first time she got sick. When it came back, I was ten. That second time, it didn't even occur to me she wouldn't beat it again. And then one day she told me she was going to the hospital again—but that she'd never come home."

"Oh, Tyler."

"And you know what I did? *I yelled at her*. I accused her of not fighting hard enough." His voice cracks. "She knew she was going to die that day, and I made her feel like she was being a terrible mom for leaving us. For leaving *me*." He turns his face away from mine and looks out the far window. He exhales a trembling breath. "When she died, I was so angry. I sat there and felt this inexplicable *rage*. I felt like God had just taken the most gigantic shit right on my head. I didn't think about my dad's pain. Or my sister's. Or even about my mom's. All I thought about was me and what I'd just lost. That nobody would ever wink at me in a rearview mirror again. Or laugh at my lame jokes. Or make me feel loved like that, ever again."

I stroke his forearm, at a loss about what to do. "I'm so sorry."

Tyler takes a deep, shuddering breath and gets himself under control. "To this day, I *hate* myself for what I put my mom through in the end. She was in horrible pain, and I didn't ease her pain. *I added to it*." He turns to look at me. He blinks and the tears pooled in his eyes course down his cheeks. "I'll never forgive myself for the things I said. And worse, the things

I *didn't* say."

I put my palm on his beautiful face. Wipe his tears. "You didn't need to say a thing to her, Tyler. She knew."

He looks down. "That's what my sister always says."

"She's right."

He doesn't reply.

"No wonder you and your sister are so close."

"I don't know what I would have done without my sister. She's always been the one who's taken care of me. Certainly not my dad."

"Why not your dad? He was grieving?"

"He couldn't function for about a year after Mom died." He pauses. "And then he found the thing to get him out of bed again. I got selected for this junior elites football team in Dallas, and he found his reason for being. And so did I. Every time I played, I knew I was saving my dad's life. Plus, I could hear my mom cheering me on. It was awesome."

"Your mom knew football?"

He nods. "Her dad was a college coach. It was in her blood. She's the one who knew I was born to be a defensive player, not my dad. Dad always thought I should be a quarterback, but Mom said, nope, I was born to hit. One day she told me I should think about being a free safety and I was like, 'But, Mom, the quarterback is the guy in charge.' And she goes, 'Honey, the free safety is the quarterback of the defense. He's the one secretly in charge. It's the defense that actually wins football games, despite appearances.' And then she showed me that famous video of Atwater taking down Okoye, and I never looked back."

"What video?"

"You know, the one where Steve Atwater puts that legendary hit on Christian Okoye?"

I look at him blankly. "I don't think I've seen that one."

"*What?*" He's absolutely appalled. "Jesus Christ, Zooey, did you grow up under a rock?"

I laugh. "Yeah, with Babar."

Tyler pulls out his phone and quickly finds the video he's talking about—the Atwater-Okoye hit of 1990. "It's only the greatest hit by a free safety in the history of the game," he says. "Maybe even the greatest hit, period. Check it out."

I look at Tyler's phone and watch a guy in a Bronco uniform—the mystery player on Tyler's wall, I immediately realize!—putting a monster hit on a running back for the Chiefs that instantly lays him out cold. "Ooph," I say, grimacing. "That had to have left a mark on poor Okoye."

Tyler tosses his phone onto the driver's seat in front of us. "To this day, I watch that hit before every game. Usually twice."

I stroke Tyler's arm. "I believe with all my heart your mom watches that video along with you. And cheers you on through every down of every game."

Tyler smiles. "I believe that, too. Same with your mom. She's there with you every time you open your mouth and unleash that angelic voice of yours."

Oh, God, my heart is bursting with love for Tyler in this moment. "Tyler?" I say quietly.

He looks at me expectantly.

"Thank you for this magical night." I put my hand on my heart. "I'll never forget it."

Tyler pulls gently on a lock of my hair, releases it, and watches it bounce and re-coil. "Zooey, I'll remember this night—and the way you're looking at me right now—as long as I live."

CHAPTER THIRTY-ONE

Tyler and I are standing at the front of our Modernizing Shakespeare class, our palms pressed together. My stomach is turning somersaults. My pulse is pounding in my ears.

"O, then, dear saint, let lips do what hands do," Tyler says, his blue eyes glinting from behind his mask. "They pray; grant thou, lest faith turn to despair."

"Saints do not move, though grant for prayers' sake," I reply, gazing deeply into Tyler's blue eyes.

"Then move not, while my prayer's effect I take," Tyler says. He cups my cheek in his free hand, leans in, and kisses me.

Oh, thank God. Tyler is smooching me precisely the way I insisted he do it. With not so much heat that everyone will know we're having sex. But with enough heat to convey Romeo's white-hot attraction to Juliet.

Now, just to be clear, if I were Tyler's girlfriend, I wouldn't mind the whole world knowing he's been screwing me. In fact, I'd take great pleasure in everyone knowing I'm the girl who somehow managed to snag God's Gift to Womankind for my very own. But under the present circumstances, when I'm figuring it's fifty-fifty Tyler and I are about to become "friends and nothing more" any minute now, I have zero desire to set myself up to look like Tyler Caldwell's fuck buddy today and pitiful cast-off tomorrow.

Tyler pulls out of our kiss and looks longingly at me. "Thus from my lips, by thine, my sin is purged."

Wow, Tyler's slaying his performance. He's no thespian, granted, but for a football player, he's damned good. "Then have my lips the sin that they have took," I reply.

"Sin from thy lips?" Tyler says smoothly. "O trespass sweetly urged! Give me my sin again." He kisses me again. But this time, he brazenly disregards my explicit instructions about the heat level of our kiss, and he devours me. *Oh, my gosh!* He's kissing the hell out of me! He's kissing me the same way he kisses me for real! *Gah!* I should pull away. People are beginning to snicker. And titter. And gasp. I can hear them. Indeed, the growing sound of our audience's extreme titillation is becoming a veritable din.

But I don't pull away. Nope. I throw my arms around Tyler's neck and return his kiss with as much passion as I can muster, eliciting whoops and applause and catcalls from our audience. Screw it. If this turns out to be our last kiss, if Tyler is going to crush me after this performance by sticking to our original arrangement, then I want every person in this room—no, every person in the world—to know that, for five glorious weeks, Tyler Caldwell and Zooey Cartwright were passionately in love. That we shared a love story that was every bit as poetic and epic...and, yes, ultimately, as *tragic*...as the love story of our star-crossed doppelgängers, Romeo and Juliet.

CHAPTER THIRTY-TWO

Tyler twirls me around in front of MacGowan Hall, almost wiping out a random student walking by with my swinging legs. "We slayed it in there!" Tyler shouts. He puts me down, laughing. But when he sees my face, his smile vanishes. "What's wrong?"

I take a deep breath. Swallow hard. "I'm just sad our projects are over, that's all. All three of them."

Tyler stares at me for a long beat. "You can't be serious."

I feel my lower lip trembling, but I can't control it. I don't reply.

"You seriously think *I* think we're over, just because we've turned in our two midterm projects?"

"I have no idea what you think," I reply honestly. "All I know is what you told me when you gave me the syllabus. And that you haven't said anything to contradict it since then."

Tyler exhales. "Come on, Zooey. We can't call it quits now. We still haven't checked off 'Fun with Food' or 'Role-play.'"

He smiles, but I remain stone-faced. If Tyler's not done with me yet simply because we haven't checked off every naughty item on his freaking syllabus, then we're most definitely not on the same page.

Tyler rakes his hand through his hair and exhales again.

LAUREN ROWE

"Shit. Okay, I guess this conversation is long overdue." He looks up at the sky for a moment and then trains his blazing blue eyes on my face. "I love you, Zooey. Okay? *I love you.* But the thing is, I've come to realize that doesn't matter."

I can't believe my ears. *He loves me?* Oh, my God! How can he possibly say that doesn't matter? *It's everything!* "I love you, too," I blurt, but it feels like a desperate plea coming out of my mouth, not something joyous. Why do I feel like he's about to punch me in the teeth?

Tyler's features soften. He takes my limp hands in his. "I know you love me, Zooey," he says softly. "You've let me know how you feel about me a thousand ways for weeks. Thank you for that. But, sweetheart, we both know love isn't going to be enough for us."

I shake my head like he's talking gibberish. "What are you talking about? I don't understand what you're saying to me."

"I'm saying we're Romeo and Juliet."

"How is that a bad thing? *Romeo and Juliet* is the greatest love story ever told."

"Babe, they both die in the end. They were star-crossed lovers. Doomed."

"Okay, then, fine. We're Jim and Pam! I don't care what you call us. We love each other."

Tyler smiles sympathetically. "No, baby. We're not Jim and Pam. I wish we were. But we're not. We're doomed, sweetheart. It's undeniable."

I open and close my mouth, utterly flabbergasted. Tears flood my eyes. "*Tyler.*"

He shakes his head. "To be honest, knowing our doomed

fate has, at times, made me want to pull away from you, just to save myself from the inevitable pain this is going to cause me. But I just can't do it. For some reason, my heart doesn't seem to care it's going to get smashed at the end of this. It just wants you for as long as it can have you."

I'm a deer in headlights. This is making absolutely no sense. "I don't understand. Why are you saying all this? No one knows the future. Nothing is set in stone."

"I know the future."

"You *don't*. No one does."

"Come on, Zooey. Think about it. Six months from now, I'm gonna get drafted top ten and immediately head off to live in whatever city takes me—and under the league's collective bargaining agreement for top picks, I'm going to be signed to a four-year deal. True, I don't know which team will select me, but the chances it'll be an LA team are almost nil. And what will you be doing for those same four years? Going to school here for at least three of them, except when you're off for summers. But during summers, I'll be away at training camp, getting my ass kicked. Explain to me when we'll have a chance to see each other for the next three to four years?"

I press my lips together.

"Plus, consider this. All those years you'll be here at school, doing your thing, you're going to be meeting lots of guys. And they're all gonna want you the same way I did when I first laid eyes on you. The same way Hanalei did. The same way Jake did. The way everyone does when they see you."

Jake? Hanalei? What?

"And maybe you're going to want some of those guys in

return, baby. Why not? You'll be nineteen, twenty years old and understandably wanting to have some fun. God knows I've had my fun in college. Lots of it. Why shouldn't you get to do that?"

"I'll never want anyone but you," I say evenly.

He smiles at me like I'm a puppy chasing my own tail. "I know you think that now, sweetheart. Thank you. But even if we somehow manage to slog through the next three or four years of an exclusive long-distance relationship during which we never see each other, we still wouldn't get our happy ending after all that suffering. After graduation, you'll be heading to New York to chase your dreams, exactly as you should. *Exactly as you've promised you'll do.* And God knows where I'll be."

I'm drowning in panic. Completely blindsided. Hyperventilating.

Out of nowhere, an epiphany slams into me, and I grasp at it like a lifeline. *TBD.* Surely, Tyler included that line item under Phase Two of the syllabus because some piece of his brain wanted to leave the tiniest opening for us to continue together past the stupid five-week mark. *Because Tyler knew in his bones we'd fall in love!* "What was TBD?" I demand, my tone much harsher than intended. By God, I'm going to use Tyler's own premonition of our love against him. I'm not going down without a fight!

Tyler stares at me blankly.

"On the syllabus," I say. "You listed TBD as the last item under Phase Two. What did it refer to?"

Tyler looks at me ruefully but doesn't speak.

"Tell me, Tyler. You knew you'd extend the five weeks even

back then, didn't you? *You knew it!*"

"It was a threesome, Zooey," Tyler says flatly. "With Jake."

I gasp.

"It was what Jake demanded to agree to swap Social Psych partners with me."

I consciously close my hanging jaw.

"Jake had seen us together on the dance floor at the party, and he assumed we'd fucked upstairs right after that. Based on what he saw of you on the dance floor, he figured you were the kind of girl who'd jump at the chance to get double-fucked by the two biggest stars on the football team." He scoffs. "Of course, I didn't tell him the real deal about you or what actually happened between us that night. I don't kiss and tell, unlike Jake the Snake." He rolls his eyes. "God, Jake's such a fucking douchebag these days, you have no idea. Ever since his break-up, Jake's been on quite the tear with the ladies. Talk about a guy who only cares about getting his dick wet."

The hair on my arms stands up.

"So, anyway, Jake wouldn't agree to switch partners with me unless I promised to ask you about the threesome idea at some point during our partnership. So I was like, 'Sure, Jake. Whatever. No promises, of course, but I'll float the idea with her when the time is right.' Honestly, Zooey, at that point, I would have said anything to get you as my partner." His eyes darken. "And, yeah, if I'm being completely honest with you, the idea of both of us fucking you back then turned me on."

"*Tyler.*"

"But all it took was our first night together, and I knew I'd never ask you about Jake. In fact, just that fast, the thought of him—or any man—laying so much as a pinky on you made me feel fucking homicidal." He clenches his jaw. His eyes are blazing. "You want to know why I've been playing like a fucking maniac since I met you? Why I've been hitting twice as hard and making twice as many tackles and interceptions as I did last year?" He cups my face in his large hands. I'm trembling in his palms. "Because when I'm playing, all I have to do is imagine the ball is *you*, and I go fucking insane whenever anyone else so much as touches it." He swallows hard. *"Because that ball is mine."*

I open my mouth and close it. *Holy shit.*

"I love you, Zooey Cartwright," Tyler says, his voice low and intense. "You're the answer to a prayer I didn't even know I had. You make me feel completely alive for the first time in my life. I'm a new man, thanks to you. Now that I've got you in my life, I can't even imagine how I'm going to be happy without you ever again. But that's exactly why I keep thinking maybe I should break things off with you now—just to save myself from getting absolutely decimated later. Let's face it, baby, the only thing loving you is going to get me in the end is a broken heart." He takes a deep, shuddering breath. His eyes are glistening and full of pain. "Zooey, baby, I've already had enough heartbreak to last me a fucking lifetime. I can't take any more."

Tears are streaming down my cheeks. He wipes them with his thumbs.

"Tyler, sweetheart, no one knows the future. Anything can happen. Think about it. Did you ever think in a million years you'd fall in love with me when you first met me at that party? And yet, here we are."

Tyler runs the pad of his thumb over my lips. "Of course, I thought I'd fall in love with you when I met you at the party. I thought I'd fall in love with you the minute I saw you. Why do you think I turned you away that first night? Babe, I felt like I'd been struck by a thunderbolt, and it scared the shit out of me."

I blink several times in rapid succession, trying to wrap my brain around that. Finally, I jut my chin at him, resolve washing over me. "Okay then. Fuck fate. If it's not our destiny to wind up together, then let the stars take their best shot at us. But in the meantime, I'm going to do everything in my power to chart my own destiny. *With you.* Our assignment was to rewrite *Romeo and Juliet* for modern times, right? Well, then, that's what we're going to do. And in our version, Romeo and Juliet are finally going to get their happily ever after."

CHAPTER THIRTY-THREE

I'm sitting in the audience at the NFL Draft in Philadelphia, along with Tyler, his dad and sister, Aaron, and Tyler's trainer and agent. And I've never been so nervous in my life. Seriously, I feel like every hair on my head is going to spontaneously fall out of my scalp any second from sheer anxiety. And that's a lot of hair, folks.

Since the first time I met Tyler at that party almost eight months ago, he's been laser-focused on this one particular day. Envisioning it. Praying about it. He's been the first player to arrive at the gym every morning and the last one to leave it in the evening. He's talked for hours on the phone with his dad to deconstruct every little thing he did right or wrong in every week's game. He's thrown himself into weight-training, running, yoga, ice baths, cryogenics, sports massages. He's studied game films, listened to motivational audiobooks, and meditated. He's foregone partying when all his teammates were getting shitfaced. And, of course, he's done the most important thing of all. He's slayed it each and every week on the playing field.

If there was something big or small Tyler Caldwell could do to position himself to get selected in the top ten of this year's draft, he's done it. And then some. And yet, as we all know too well, nothing in life is guaranteed—especially when it comes to the business of football.

So far, the first four picks in the draft have been a defensive end from Texas A&M, an offensive tackle from Clemson, a quarterback from Alabama, and another offensive tackle from LSU. The Miami Dolphins are currently on the clock, with about two minutes remaining before the commissioner announces their first-round pick—the fifth overall selection in the draft.

God, please let Miami pick Tyler.

The Dolphins aren't Tyler's dream team, of course. The Cowboys are. But childhood fantasies mean jack squat to Tyler right now—this is business. Under the league's collective bargaining agreement, the salaries for the top twenty draft picks are predetermined right down the line. The number one pick is guaranteed a package worth over fifty million bucks, the number two guy gets a deal worth over forty-eight million, and so on. Sitting here right now, we know for certain if Tyler is drafted fifth, he'll sign a four-year deal worth over forty-one million bucks, fifteen million of it up front in the form of a signing bonus. If Tyler goes sixth instead of fifth, his deal will be worth a whopping four million less. If he goes seventh, he'll lose another four mil. And so on. Needless to say, Tyler's hoping the commissioner announces his name next.

Oh, God, the commissioner is headed to the lectern at the front of the large conference center. Out of nowhere, a guy with a large camera with ESPN on its side appears next to Tyler, primed and ready to capture Tyler's reaction if indeed his name is called next.

Tyler slides his hand into mine and squeezes. I open my mouth to say something encouraging and realize there's nothing to say. I hold my breath and pray and pray and pray on a running loop inside my head that fickle Fortune will smile on my beloved Tyler today.

"With the fifth pick," the commissioner says into his microphone. Tyler squeezes my hand even harder. "The Miami Dolphins select... *Tyler Caldwell*, free safety, UCLA."

The place erupts in loud cheers.

Tyler leaps to his feet and fist-pumps the air. He looks up, points to the sky, and blows a kiss to heaven—a simple gesture that instantly brings tears to my eyes. He hugs his dad *hard*, and I'm shocked to see his normally stoic father crying like a baby. His sister joins her father and brother in a three-way hug for a poignant moment, and my heart squeezes at the thought of the loss those three have endured. And then Tyler gets to me.

He picks me up, kisses me on the lips, and whispers into my ear, "Top five is because I've got my lucky beaver-charm with me today." He kisses me a second time, puts me down, and quickly moves on to embrace Aaron. After quick hugs with his trainer and agent, he's off, marching in his tailored suit toward the humongous stage at the front of the massive room with that cameraman in tow. I clutch my heart as I watch my beloved Tyler bounding gleefully through the crowd, getting patted and bro-hugged by everyone as he goes. Finally, Tyler makes it to the stage and effusively accepts an aqua and orange Miami Dolphins jersey from the commissioner. He holds it up for an army of photographers, his smile at full wattage.

And what am I doing? Crying. Squealing. Clutching my heart. Shaking. Gasping. Smiling bigger than I've ever smiled in my life. And, if I'm being honest, through it all, I'm also simultaneously marveling that a girl can feel this purely and unconditionally elated for the man she loves, even though she knows without a doubt the stars that have been hovering over her and her lover's heads for the past six months just now... indisputably...*crossed.*

CHAPTER THIRTY-FOUR

"Crash into Me" is playing on low volume as Tyler slowly makes love to me on top of our fluffy hotel bed. I figured after the thrill of Tyler's top five selection today, he'd be so amped, we'd go back to our hotel room and fuck like monkeys to celebrate. But, nope. It seems after this exciting and surreal day, Tyler wants to celebrate his triumph by reveling in my body with slow and sensuous strokes. And I'm not complaining.

Tyler pulls my arms above my head, clasps my fingers in his, and kisses me deeply as his hips move deliciously on top of mine. "So glad you're here with me," he whispers, his voice husky.

I squeeze Tyler's fingers in mine, close my eyes, and inhale, taking in his masculine scent. Ah, yes, that's the drug, baby. It's the scent that makes me pilfer Tyler's lightly worn T-shirts from his hamper and wear them to bed whenever we're apart.

Tyler reaches down between our bodies and massages my swollen tip as he slides in and out of me. "You're my lucky beaver-charm, pretty baby," he whispers as his fingers work me.

A moment later, I climax, gritting out Tyler's name as I do, and shortly thereafter, he growls and shudders on top of me with a release of his own.

After some tender kissing, Tyler rolls off me and we lie together, nose to nose. We talk about the unbelievable day. About how shocked and touched we both were when his dad cried. About how Tyler doesn't even remember walking up to that stage after his name was called. And then, out of nowhere, I think I detect anxiety flickering across Tyler's beautiful face.

"Is something wrong?" I ask.

"I'm just wondering when rehearsals start for you. Sorry. I know you already told me. I can't keep anything straight."

Two weeks ago, I auditioned for the lead role in UCLA's spring-quarter mainstage production of *Carrie*, a musical based on the book and movie of the same name. And much to my shock, I got the part. I hadn't expected to get into the show at all, let alone to be cast as Carrie herself. I'd only auditioned to get some auditioning experience. But that's life for you. Sometimes, it'll shock you.

"My first rehearsal is Monday," I reply, and the minute the words leave my mouth, I regret taking the role. Now that Tyler and I have only a few weeks together before he'll have to leave for Miami, I want to spend every possible minute of them with him.

"That's great," Tyler says. "I'm glad you'll have something to keep you extra busy."

"No, it's terrible," I reply. "Rehearsals are going to cut into our time together before you leave. Did they give you a firm date for when you need to report for camp?"

That same anxiety from a moment ago flickers across Tyler's face again. "Yeah. Um. It turns out there's a rookie mini-camp next week."

My heart stops. "*Next week?*"

"And then there's a full rookie camp a couple weeks after that. Followed by training camp for the entire team in July. I'm sure I'll be able to get back to LA to see every performance of your show. But that's probably going to be the last time I'll be able to get to LA 'til January."

I can't believe it. I was counting on having *weeks* with Tyler before he had to leave for training camp in Miami. I wasn't mentally prepared for him to leave *next week*. "So we've only got a week before you have to leave?"

Tyler twists his mouth. "Actually, uh, I've got to head to Miami..." He takes a deep breath. "I've got to head out there in three days, Zooey."

Time stops. I can't breathe. "*Three days?*" I choke out.

"Just enough time for me to head back to LA with you, pack a bag, and fly back out."

Tears threaten but I force them down. Tyler doesn't need to see me fall apart. Not today. Not ever, actually. Today, his dream, the dream he's shared with his father his entire life, the dream he believes his mother would have wanted for him, has finally come true. The impact of his dream fulfillment on our relationship is irrelevant, and I know it. I came here to support him and to be thrilled for him, come what may, and that's what I'm going to do. "Sounds exciting," I manage to say brightly. "How long will you be out there?"

He looks stressed. "I don't know how long I'll be gone on this first trip. While I'm in Miami, I'm gonna have to start looking for a place to live. I'll definitely come back and see your show, for sure, like I said, but shortly after that, I've got to get settled into my new...home."

Home. Such a loaded word. But it's the right one, isn't it? Tyler won't be visiting Miami. He'll be living there for God knows how long. Maybe even forever.

Tyler touches my cheek. "I'm sorry, baby."

"I'll apply to the University of Miami," I blurt, panic descending upon me. "I'm sure they've got a theater program there. And if they don't, then I'll study, I don't know, English or communications."

For a long moment, Tyler doesn't react to my outburst, other than to gently stroke my hair like he's calming a stray dog at the pound. "You can't move to Miami, beaver," he finally says. "You'd be miserable there."

"I'll be even more miserable without you."

"And what about your scholarship to UCLA?" he asks. "You don't care about that? If you think I'm gonna pay your way at U of Miami with all my millions, you're sorely mistaken, you mooch." He smiles.

I blink back tears. "But I don't remember how to be happy without you, Tyler."

Pain washes over Tyler's face. "You've got a destiny to fulfill, sweetheart. Every bit as much as I do. We both know that. We've always known it."

I stare at him for a very long time, my lower lip trembling. He's right. My brain knows he is. My dreams require me to eventually wind up in New York, not Miami. But my heart simply doesn't want to accept today's triumph will likely be our undoing. "Can I come visit you this summer?"

"I'll be at training camp this summer. You know that."

I hang my head, defeated. "I'm sorry. I'm honestly elated for you. The three-days thing just threw me for a loop."

"Babe, I know you're elated for me. There's no doubt in my mind about that." He pulls me into him and I crumple, literally and figuratively, against his hard chest.

He wraps his strong arms around me, and I clutch him to me while Dave Matthews serenades us with his soulful, bittersweet song. And for the first time ever—even though by this time I've heard "Crash into Me" more times than I can count—it suddenly occurs to me how eerily prescient Tyler's selection of this particular song was all those months ago. This beautiful boy crashed into me like a ton of bricks from the moment I first laid eyes on him. And now, it seems, fickle Fate is demanding I finally suffer the inevitable...*burn*.

CHAPTER THIRTY-FIVE

Tyler puts down his carry-on suitcase and hugs me one last time before heading into the airport security line. "Don't forget to send me photos from rehearsals," he says. "I want to see your costumes. Oh, and the first time they drench you in blood at rehearsal, you'd better Snapchat me that shit or I'll never forgive you."

"Only if you promise to send me a selfie when you've got your full Dolphins uniform on for the first time. I want to see your name on the back."

He looks like he's getting choked up.

I touch his cheek. "Babe, there's no crying in football."

He nods.

"I'm just a text or phone call away. Any time you want to talk, I'll be here. Any time you want to watch an episode of *The Office* with me on FaceTime, I'm in. Any episode you want, as long as it's not from season eight or from before Pam and Jim get together."

"Well, duh. I'm not a complete moron, Zooey."

We share a sad smile.

I lift my face to him, and he presses his lips against mine. "I love you, beaver," he whispers. "I'll love you as long as I live. Always know that."

I swallow the lump in my throat. "Please don't say it like that. It makes it seem like this is goodbye forever. It's not. I'm coming to your first game, remember? And I'm sure I can make it to games you play on the west coast. And there's always Thanksgiving and Christmas breaks. This isn't goodbye."

I don't know why I'm babbling like this. We've already talked about all this, several times. And when we did, we both came to the stark realization the actual opportunities for us to see each other will be so few and far between, and likely so short and unsatisfying when they do occur, they might actually feel more heartbreaking than uplifting. In fact, after we looked hard at the reality of the situation, it was me who suggested we shouldn't be exclusive any more. It's just too hard to make long-term commitments when we know Tyler will probably be in Miami for the next four years at least, and I'll be here in LA, followed by chasing my Broadway dreams. And so, we've made the mature and rational decision to be friends who love each other deeply and who might get to see each other on special occasions and quite happily fuck each other's brains out when they do. But we are officially no longer in a committed relationship. And we are officially *not* going to be sad about it, because this new chapter in our lives came about thanks to Tyler's lifelong dreams coming true. Which is totally and completely awesome.

"You'd better go," I say. "You don't want to be late for your flight."

Tyler nods. "Oh, hey, I almost forgot. Look at this nifty shirt I had made for the occasion." He unzips his fleece to reveal the phrase I Love Beaver! emblazoned across his broad chest.

I'm aghast. "*Tyler.*" I look around, half expecting someone from TMZ to pop out from behind a luggage cart and snap a photo. "Cover that up, babe. Someone might see."

He laughs.

"Thanks for the sentiment, but you can't wear that. Someone will take a photo, and it'll go viral and the whole world will think Tyler Caldwell is the biggest douchebag pervert sexist in the world."

Tyler chuckles again.

"I'm not kidding, love. Your branding is really important now. You're on a national stage. You have to think about that kind of thing now."

"Relax, little freshman, I've got a change of shirts in my bag. I just wanted to see you freak out over it. Mission accomplished."

"Very funny." I bite my lip. "And very sweet. Thank you."

"It's yet another instance of our elephant wearing his elephant T-shirt, don't you think?" He winks at me and zips up his fleece again. "Seriously, I'm a genius with this T-shirt thing. Just watch. It's gonna be huge."

"No doubt." I kiss him. "Text me when you land so I know you're safe."

"I will." He touches my hair. Pulls on a strand and watches it spring back. "God, I'm gonna miss this beautiful hair."

I take a deep, steadying breath. My only job today is to keep our farewell light and bright so he can walk onto that airplane feeling nothing but excitement about this new chapter of his life. "I'll miss this superhero chin," I say, touching his steel chin with my fingertip. "But I'll be happy knowing you're doing what you were born to do. No matter what happens, one day we'll look back on the twists and turns of our lives and say, 'I wouldn't change a thing because it got me to where I am right now, and right now is fucking awesome.' You'll see. Everything happens for a reason. I firmly believe that."

Tyler bites his cheek.

"So get on that plane and kick some ass and enjoy every minute of this crazy ride. You've worked too hard not to enjoy the fruits of your labor."

For a split second, Tyler looks like he's stuffing down tears. But he takes a deep breath and regains control. "I'll text you when I land." With that, he kisses my cheek, picks up his suitcase, and strides with purpose into the security line.

For the next few minutes, I stand frozen watching him, even though all he's doing is standing in a security line with his back to me. I know it's stupid, but I need to see his face one last time before I can leave, even if it's just in profile.

Finally, Tyler reaches the front of the line. He shows his ID and boarding pass to the TSA officer and, thank God, as he does, I get a glimpse of his handsome profile. The officer waves Tyler through and he walks toward the screening area. But just before Tyler gets to the entryway to the screening area, he surprises me by turning completely around and searching the crowd.

Our eyes lock.

Tyler flashes me a crooked smile, and I touch my heart. He makes a face like, *Can you believe this?* and I laugh and nod. *Yes, I can.* A nearby TSA agent says something to Tyler, and he nods at the woman. But his gaze immediately returns to me. He graces me with one last, heartbreaking smile and a palm pressed against his heart. And then he turns around, walks through the entryway to the screening area, and disappears.

I stand rooted to my spot for a long time, irrationally thinking he might pop through the entryway again. But, of course, he doesn't. He's gone.

"O, I am Fortune's fool," I whisper softly.

My shoulders drooping, I turn on my heel and begin walking through swarms of travelers, feeling like I'm trudging through molasses. After about ten steps, I stop short, my breathing too ragged and my vision too blurred by tears to continue. I stumble to a nearby bench and plop myself down, a deer in headlights. One more glance at the entryway where Tyler disappeared only moments ago and the bottomless sorrow I've been stuffing down for three solid days lurches out of my mouth and pours out of me in the form of racking, wretched sobs.

CHAPTER THIRTY-SIX

"Can I borrow some of your rouge, Zo?" one of my fellow cast members asks, pointing to a palette of stage makeup on the table in front of me.

"Sure thing, baby." I slide it over to her.

It's Sunday. About an hour and a half before the start of our matinee performance in... Where are we again? Oh, yeah. *Appleton, Wisconsin.* And I'm sitting next to one of my best friends in the *Wicked* cast in the communal dressing room assigned to us lowly chorus members. All around me, fellow chorus members are getting ready for the show, totally invading each other's personal space as they do. But that's just the way it is with a traveling production; everyone has to be willing to kiss their personal space goodbye because you never know how big or small the dressing rooms might be in any particular theater. And, frankly, the surprise of each new city is half the fun. Even some of the suckiest things about the grind of performing in a touring show—the stuff the veterans in the cast seem to gripe about the most—seem like a grand adventure to me.

I'm just starting to apply my eyeliner when a reminder goes off on my phone, telling me it's time to text Tyler before his one o'clock game. I grab my phone and tap out a text.

Good luck in your game, Mr. God's Gift to Womankind.Rip their heads off, you savage beast!

I add a football, dolphin, and aqua and orange hearts to my message and press Send. It's more or less the same pregame text I've been sending to Tyler since my very first text to him well over two years ago, back when I was nothing but Tyler's five-week miseducation project. Minus the dolphin and aqua and orange hearts, of course. Back in the day, I used to send Tyler a little bear, a football, and *blue* and *gold* hearts with whatever message. But, otherwise, it's essentially the same text.

And my text isn't the only thing that's remained constant when it comes to Tyler. Since I first plastered a smile on my face and said goodbye to Tyler at the airport over a year and a half ago, my heart has never stopped being his. In fact, I can honestly say I love Tyler now more than ever. Unfortunately, though, I've come to realize in all this time he was right all along. Loving him doesn't change our fate.

Tyler's meteoric rise in Miami happened exactly the way I would have scripted it if I'd been writing the movie of his life. Last year, he wound up having a stellar rookie season that far exceeded everyone's expectations of him. And that's saying a lot, seeing as how football organizations and fans tend to have extremely high expectations of a guy being paid forty-one million bucks. And now, in the middle of Tyler's second season, he's performing even better than he did last year. In fact, thanks to Tyler and some other notable impact players the Dolphins acquired in the off-season, the formerly abysmal

Dolphins have more than a snowball's chance at making the playoffs at the end of this year.

Of course, thanks to Tyler's stellar play and good looks and larger-than-life personality off the field, not to mention his omnipresent message T-shirts, Tyler's become a huge fan favorite, and not just in the greater Miami area. He's a star across the entire country. And it all started when Tyler showed up for his first press conference as a rookie wearing a shirt that read "This is what God CALD a job WELL done!" Those first images of him looking so gorgeous and cocky went completely viral, and a star was instantly born. And the best part? Tyler had already gotten that catchphrase and a bunch of others trademarked the prior year, which meant when Nike came calling toward the end of his rookie season to propose a global line of "Tyler Caldwell" brand sportswear, he was in the driver's seat.

And now, here we are. After a season and a half in the NFL, Tyler's already one of the league's most recognizable and valuable players. When Tyler's sportswear line launched this past summer, it was an instant smash. Plus, he's a featured face in Nike's latest ad campaign, a series of glossy commercials showing Tyler and other highly attractive athletes shirtless and full of muscles in black and white, working out while sweat drips down their glorious muscles. Seriously, it's hard to figure out what they're trying to sell in those ads besides sex. Not that I'm complaining. Tyler in particular looks like a freaking wet dream in those commercials. They're one tick shy of soft porn. So, yeah, needless to say, Tyler's quickly attracted a massive fan base in record time. Which has led to even more commercials and ads for products like cologne and watches and suits and cars and celebrity fashion shows for charity. Which means Tyler's not hurting for cash these days. Or adulation, both of the male and female varieties.

Speaking of female adulation...I don't know if Tyler's dated anyone while he's been in Miami this past year and a half. If he has, he's had the good sense not to mention it to me. He certainly hasn't been photographed with anyone. If he had been, I would have seen the photo by now. Because I've been looking. Hard.

For my part, I've had no interest in dating anyone else, though I've certainly had plenty of opportunities both at school and here on the road. The first and only time I kissed someone else, just out of curiosity, my stomach revolted and I instantly realized, if I can't have Tyler, I'd rather just be alone. At least for now. Obviously, I can't be alone forever. But I just can't seem to move on from Tyler. Not when my heart still belongs to him so completely. When it comes to Tyler, it's like my heart is bursting with joy and panging with emptiness, all at the same time. It's wonderful and horrible, all at once.

It was only when I accepted this job with the official traveling production of *Wicked* almost six months ago, right after the end of my second year at UCLA, that I finally found myself leaping out of bed every morning again, the same way I used to do before Tyler left for Miami. Before I got this job, I went about the business of my second year of school, including throwing myself into all sorts of new activities. I got cast in the Spring Sing. That was awesome. I went to football games to cheer on Aaron and Hanalei. Hung out a ton with Clarissa and Dimitri, who are as cute together as ever. And, of course, I studied like crazy, too. But, through it all, I always felt like I was missing a limb. Was I happy? Sure. Most of the time. But never *completely*.

On the few occasions when Tyler and I saw each other during his rookie year, we always picked right back up where we'd left off, both emotionally and physically. But while those short reunions were wonderful and amazing at the time, they were torturous, too. Each and every goodbye became harder and harder on us both. It was like we kept wrapping bandages around our broken hearts only to take a sledgehammer to them right afterward.

Just when I felt like my heart couldn't bear another swing from the sledgehammer, the off-season arrived, and Tyler came to stay in LA for four solid months. And our hearts mended. We were as in love as ever before.

And then, dang it, June rolled around. School ended. Tyler left for Miami again. So I got a waitressing job and went to a slew of auditions, just for the heck of it...and immediately landed this job right out of the gate. Of course, I was over the moon about it...until I found out the job would require a *nine-month* commitment, not the three months I'd originally thought. Which meant I'd have to take a year's leave of absence from school to take the job. Not that big a deal, actually. But it also meant Tyler and I wouldn't be able to spend his second off-season together. And that wasn't okay with me. Not at all.

But Tyler was adamant I take the job. In fact, he wouldn't hear of me turning it down. And my dad was surprisingly encouraging about it, too, especially when he found out the pay was two thousand per week plus a *per diem* for food and lodging. Plus, two professors both told me accepting the job was an absolute no-brainer. "You'll learn more on tour for nine months than you would in a classroom for three full years," one of my professors said.

And so, I took the damned job.

And I've been on the road ever since.

The last time I saw Tyler was about a month ago in Boston. He came to see the show during his bye-week and stayed with me for two nights at the swankiest hotel I've ever been in. And, of course, our time together was amazing, as always. But when it was time to say goodbye that time, I sobbed harder than ever—so hard, my eyes swelled shut. I begged Tyler to let me move to Miami, but he said no. He'd seen me onstage three times in two days and said he'd never seen my face light up that way before. I protested, but Tyler firmly shot me down. "If you moved to Miami, you'd eventually hold it against me for keeping you from your soul's destiny. And then we'd be doomed, regardless."

And that was that. I didn't fight him. Because, to my shame, a part of me knew he was right.

My phone buzzes on my makeup table, pulling me out of my thoughts. It's a reply from Tyler to my "good luck in your game" text from earlier.

Can you talk for a minute, Zo?

I'm shocked. Tyler rarely replies to my "good luck" texts before games. He almost always waits until afterward. And he's never once in two years asked to talk to me before a game.

To the contrary, Tyler always prefers to shut out the world and retreat into his own mind before every game. I text him.

Everything okay?

Just want to hear your voice. Big game today.

I'll call in 2 secs. Need to go somewhere quiet.

I bolt out of the dressing room, find a quiet spot, and place the call.

"Hey," Tyler says when he picks up my call.

"Are you okay?"

"Just wanted to hear your voice."

"You're sure you're okay?"

"Just wanted to talk to my good luck charm for a minute. It's a big game."

"Why is today such a big game?"

"Every game is do-or-die from here on out for us. But, you know, one game at a time."

"Do-or-die is good. You thrive under pressure."

"True. So where are you?"

"The epicenter of the western world, Appleton, Wisconsin."

"*Nice.*" He chuckles. "You gonna be watching my game today?"

Wow. Yet another question Tyler has never asked me before a game. "Just the first quarter," I admit. "Sundays we've got a matinee, remember? But don't worry, I'll watch whatever I missed on NFL streaming before my evening show. That's what I always do when I miss one of your games—I stream it later."

"You do? Do you watch the entire game or just the highlights?"

"The whole thing. Every play. I've never once missed a single minute of any of your games, Tyler. I might have to watch a game after the fact, but I always see every second of every game at some point."

"I had no idea. I thought you just watched the highlights. Wow. Thanks." He pauses. "So are they begging you to be Elphaba yet?"

I chuckle. "No, Tyler. Not even a little bit. Our Elphaba is phenomenal."

"You're way better than she is."

"She's not the Elphaba you saw in Boston. This one joined the show a couple weeks ago. She used to be Elphaba on Broadway before she had a baby, and now she's back. She's incredible. The best one I've ever seen."

"I don't need to see her perform to know you're better than she is. Nobody is better than my beaver."

"She's better than me."

"Not possible."

"I'm learning, though. Getting to watch this woman perform every night has taught me so much. I feel like I'm going to be ready to kick some serious ass when I get my chance one day."

"Of course you are. So why'd the Boston Elphaba leave? Was she tired of looking like a chump onstage next to Zooey Cartwright for three hours every night?"

"Yeah. That's why she left. She was shown up by some anonymous curly-haired girl waaaaaaay in the back of the chorus. Either that or she landed the lead role in *Waitress* on Broadway. It was one or the other."

"They should have made you Elphaba when the Boston Elphaba left. They're idiots."

"Patience, eager beaver," I say. "I'm a wee little freshman in this world. I'm still learning and earning my stripes."

"Good girl," he says softly. "Keep earning those stripes, pretty baby."

My heart pangs. God, I hate it when his voice sounds all wistful like that. It makes me want to drop everything and go to him, no matter what he says.

"I've got to go," he declares. "Make sure you keep your eyes glued to the TV during the first quarter. Now that I know you'll be watching, I'll do everything in my power to get an interception for you while you're watching live."

"Ooooh, Tyler Caldwell's calling his shot," I say. "I tell you what. Get me that interception and I'll send you a dirty video tonight."

"Oooooh, now there's a girl who knows how to motivate a guy." He chuckles. "Will this dirty video involve my beaver's beaver, hopefully?"

I smile into the phone. If this is how we do "we've both agreed we're not in a committed relationship anymore," then we truly suck at it. "It will. My beaver will be front and center and open wide."

"Consider that interception already in the books."

I sigh into the phone. "Good luck. I'll be sending you all

my positive juju."

"Good luck to you, too, baby. Or, rather, break a leg."

"Thanks. And, please, for the love of God, don't you do the same."

"No worries. Tyler Caldwell is invincible."

I chuckle. Yep, it's definitely game day—the one day of the week Tyler talks about himself in third person.

"I'll text you after I've watched the full game," I say.

"Call me, instead. Win or lose, I'll want to hear your voice."

My heart skips a beat. *What is this?* Yet another first. "Okay. I will."

"I'll talk to you later, sweetheart," he whispers. "Bye."

"Bye, cupcake. Talk to you later."

We hang up.

I love you, Tyler.

I text him a little football followed by a heart, and two seconds later, he replies with his usual text to me—a beaver and a heart. Well, actually, it's not *technically* a beaver. It's a squirrel. But I know exactly what Tyler means, without him needing to explain it to me. There's no beaver on the emoji menu, so that beautiful boy is simply making do as best he can.

CHAPTER THIRTY-SEVEN

I lean forward toward the TV screen. We're seven minutes into the first quarter. The Chargers' pass was tipped at the line, and now it's gracelessly wobbling through the air. Out of nowhere, Tyler leaps across the screen, a blur of aqua and orange.

Tyler comes down with the ball, and I squeal with glee. He's on the run, cradling the ball in his bent arm. He dodges a running back's sorry excuse for a tackle. And then an offensive lineman's. Finally, he makes the quarterback look like a fool, son! And now he's free and clear and streaking down the sideline toward the Promised Land...*Touchdown!*

Tyler's teammates converge on him in the end zone. But just before they reach him, Tyler turns directly to the nearest camera, brings the football horizontally up to his facemask, and moves it back and forth across his face like he's gnawing voraciously on it.

I clutch my heart. *Oh, my God.*

The TV commentator laughs uproariously. "What in the heck is Tyler Caldwell doing? Eating corn on the cob?"

"Maybe he's telling the world he's eating the Chargers for lunch," the other commentator suggests.

"See, this is a perfect example of why I'm so glad they've

relaxed the 'no celebration' rule in the NFL," the first commentator says. "Football should be fun, for Pete's sake. It's entertainment. And nobody knows how to entertain better than Tyler Caldwell. That guy..."

I've stopped listening. Indeed, I've stopped breathing. *That was it. My sign.* All this time, I've been waiting for a sign from the universe that our time had finally arrived. That suddenly, things would click for Tyler and me and become easy. But, out of nowhere, I understand that to make this work, Tyler and I are going to have to take matters into our own hands. That it's not going to be easy. It's going to be hard. And that's okay. Screw waiting for the stars to uncross themselves. Fuck the stars. Tyler and I love each other. And that's all that matters. Easy. Hard. It doesn't matter. We're meant to be.

"Zooey!" my castmate calls to me, popping her head into the small sitting room. "Show time!"

I turn off the TV with a shaky hand. *Yes.* I'm going to go out on that stage and perform in this matinee and the minute I get offstage, I'm going to call Tyler and tell him what I've decided. He's mine and I'm his, and it's always been that way and always will be. I want him and no one else, and nothing else matters. Let the chips fall where they may. When my contract is done in three months, I'm not going to renew. I'm going to move to Miami and live with the love of my life and have faith the rest will take care of itself. New York is only a three-hour flight from Miami, for crying out loud. I don't need to give up on my dreams to be with the man of my dreams. *I just need to be willing to commute.*

CHAPTER THIRTY-EIGHT

I practically sprint offstage after the curtain call and beeline to the dressing room. I can't wait to call Tyler and tell him about my preshow epiphany. Before calling, though, I click into the ESPN app on my phone and check the final score of his game. *Shit*. The Dolphins lost in overtime by three points.

"Damn," I whisper softly.

I click on a link to see an overview of the game highlights and gasp at the horrific words on my screen.

> *FS Tyler Caldwell injured 2nd quarter. Knee. Torn MCL and ACL. Confirmed out for remainder of season.*

I burst into tears. "*Tyler*. Oh, my God, no."

CHAPTER THIRTY-NINE

I walk quietly into the hospital room, my stomach twisted into vicious knots. Tyler's lying on top of a metal-framed bed, his muscular body splayed out. He's got some sort of motorized contraption on his left knee. His dad and sister are sitting in a corner, looking wiped out while Tyler listens intently to some guy in a white lab coat speaking to him in hushed tones. I can only imagine what dire things the guy is saying to Tyler—from what I've been able to find out from Google, more often than not, Tyler's type of knee injury is career-ending for most professional football players.

At my movement at the door, Tyler's eyes flicker to me. Instantly, emotion washes over his face. I bolt toward him, promising myself for the hundredth time I won't fall apart in his presence. When I reach him, I hug him fiercely, but he stiffens in my arms. I pull back, perplexed, and realize my touch has triggered a tsunami of emotion inside him—emotion he doesn't want to release in the presence of anyone but me.

"Can Zooey and I have a minute?" Tyler chokes out.

The minute we're alone, I hug Tyler to me and instantly, he breaks down in my arms.

I hold him as his tears flow. "If anyone can overcome this, it's you," I assure him as he quakes against me. "I did some research, love. This is going to be hard, but not impossible. *This isn't the end, Tyler.*"

He doesn't reply.

"I'm here, baby. I'm not going anywhere," I whisper softly. "We'll do this together. I'll be with you every step of the way. I love you. Only you. Always you. Forever. You matter more to me than anything in the world. We'll do this together."

Tyler wipes his eyes and slowly calms down. "I've been missing you so much lately, baby. I was having a hard time."

"Is that why you wanted to hear my voice today?"

He nods. "When they were carting me off the field today, I knew right then my knee was blown. And I thought, Now you don't have football or the love of your life. Nice work, dumbfuck."

I burst into tears. "You've got me, Tyler. You always have. I've never stopped being yours. I haven't been with anyone else. Not once."

He looks relieved. "I haven't been with anyone else, either."

Elation surges inside me. I throw myself at him again and pepper his salty cheeks with kisses. "I know it feels hopeless right now. But you'll defy the odds." I touch his tear-streaked face. "You'll defy gravity, my love. You always have and always will."

Tyler doesn't reply. He just gazes at me, looking absolutely spent.

"Normal rules don't apply to you," I say softly, stroking his hair. "Yes, this injury takes some guys down for the count. But they're not *you*. I researched it and there are a handful of guys who've come back from this exact injury, better than ever. One guy played, like, nine years after coming back. You'll be like him."

Tyler still doesn't reply.

I stroke his hair. "I love you."

He takes a deep breath. "I love you, too."

"Good. I'm glad we've got that settled. Now let's do this, okay? Positive thoughts from here on out. Failure isn't an option."

Tyler lets out a long, exhausted sigh. He pulls a strand of my hair taut and then watches it coil back into place upon release. "Thank you for coming, baby. I needed you."

"Of course, love. We're a team."

He wipes his eyes and exhales. Clenches his jaw. "Okay. Let's do this."

CHAPTER FORTY

The room is filled with the low sounds of the UCLA football game on TV and the motorized hum of the high-tech ice pack strapped to Tyler's knee. Surgery to repair Tyler's torn MCL three days ago went well, or so it seems. It's too early to know for sure. And now Tyler's on doctor's orders to rest and recover for a few months until it's time for a second surgery to repair his torn ACL.

I'm currently lying next to Tyler in his bed at his beachside home in Miami. My eyes are closed, but I'm not even close to falling asleep. I'm just sort of letting my mind wander, thinking about what I want to say in my admissions essay to the University of Miami. I've done some research, and it turns out they have a well-regarded musical theater program. Who knew? So I'm thinking I'll go back to being a college girl, this time in Miami, while Tyler recovers and trains his ass off for his comeback, which should take place in about a year or so. Knock on wood. Of course, I've got to get admitted to UM for this little plan of mine to work, but the admissions numbers on their website indicate I'm a shoe-in.

I'm actually kind of excited about going back to school. Getting to watch those veteran performers every night on tour made me realize I've still got a whole lot to learn before I could even think about holding down the lead in a Broadway-caliber show. No matter what happens in the future, even if I wind up spending the next five years here in Miami with Tyler and never stepping foot onto a professional stage during that time, this plan will nonetheless allow me to learn and grow and better myself as a performer and person. Plus, I'll maybe perform in some college productions, and that will help me keep my performing chops up for when I'll hopefully grace a professional stage one day again. All things considered, I think it's a perfect plan.

My phone pings next to me on the bed. I pick it up, look at it, and quickly put it down again.

"Who was that?" Tyler asks.

"My stage manager."

"What did she say?"

"She was just checking in."

"But what specifically did she say?"

"She said the policy is one week off for family emergencies, and she wants to know if I'm coming back in two days or not. If not, she said she's sorry but she needs to fill my spot."

"Are you going to text her back?"

"I'll call her in a minute. I'm in the middle of thinking brilliant thoughts over here."

"What are you going to tell her when you call?"

I turn my head and look at Tyler, surprised he's asking the question. "That I'm leaving the tour."

Tyler furrows his brow. "You sure about that?"

I make a face like that's a patently ridiculous question. "Of course."

"Let's talk it through. Make sure you're making the right decision."

"There's nothing to talk about. I'm not leaving you. We're a team now."

Tyler twists his mouth. "Zooey, my gut tells me you shouldn't break your contract. Your word is your bond. It's not professional to leave them hanging."

I'm stunned. "I know, but it can't be helped." I motion to his knee.

"But breaking your first ever touring contract because your boyfriend hurt his knee might give you a bad rep in the industry. You don't want to get yourself blacklisted. You might never get hired for a Broadway-quality tour like this again."

I truly can't believe my ears. "Tyler, this situation isn't as simple as 'my boyfriend hurt his knee.' Obviously."

"But that's how they'll see it. For them, this is business. You signed a contract, and you're not honoring it because, waah, waah, your football-player boyfriend hurt his knee. They'll think you're unreliable and flaky and that you don't honor your commitments."

"I don't care if they think I'm the world's biggest flake. I'm not leaving you."

He sighs and looks up at the ceiling for a moment. "You loved being on that tour."

"Yeah, well, I love being with you more."

"That's what you think at twenty. But how will you feel about this decision when you're thirty, and the window of opportunity to get a professional theater career going has closed?"

I open and close my mouth, not sure how to answer that question.

"Look, I know we've been going on and on about how I'm gonna stage a comeback in a year. And I appreciate your positivity. It fires me up. But nothing's guaranteed in football. We both know that. Anything could happen. Even if I do wind up coming back better than ever at some point, I'm still looking at best-case scenario eight more years in the league. Probably much less than that, statistically." He motions to his knee. "Or maybe, thanks to this, I'll never play again. We just don't know. But guess what I do know for sure? I want to be with you for the rest of my life. And the last thing I want you to do is look back when you're thirty or forty or fifty and have any regrets about what you gave up for me at twenty."

I sigh with frustration. "Tyler, this is a pointless conversation. I'm not leaving you to return to the tour. There will be other tours. Like you said, I'm twenty."

"But you never know how one decision can torpedo you. My gut says breaking this contract might be a game-changer in a bad way. The thing you look back on and regret the most."

"I'll have to take that chance. If they think I'm a contract-breaking flake, I can't help that. There's no way I'm leaving you to go back on the road for three whole months. Your mental health is part of your recovery. You need companionship. Optimism. I'm not going to desert you in your time of need." I pat his arm. "Don't worry about me, baby. I've already figured out a brilliant plan for me to have my cake and eat it, too. I'm going to apply to the U of Miami. It turns out they have a great musical theater program. Who knew?"

I'm expecting Tyler's face to light up at my idea, but he looks wary. He sighs. Furrows his brow. Looks up at the ceiling. And then his face lights up with an unmistakable epiphany. "Why don't I come with you on tour?"

I stare at him blankly, not able to process the bizarre words that just came out of his mouth.

"Why not?" he continues, looking increasingly energized by the idea. "For the next few months, I'm on doctor's orders to rest up. Well, shit, I can rest up in five-star hotels from Oklahoma to New Mexico just as easily as I can do it here. If I need physical therapy or whatever during that time, then I'll hire someone to travel with me. Easy peasy. Top hotels always have pretty good fitness centers."

I clutch my throat, flabbergasted. "You'd do that for me?"

Tyler's eyes are positively sparkling. "Hell yeah. The more I think about it, being on tour with you would be a whole lot better for my mental health than lying around here and feeling sorry for myself. I'll use the time to design some kick-ass T-shirts. Maybe get started on putting together that charitable foundation I've been thinking about starting. Maybe I'll scope out some new real estate investments. Work out every morning in the hotel gym. Plus, I'll get to see dazzling places like Appleton, Wisconsin, up close and personal. And best of all, I'll get to watch my little beaver perform every evening, twice on Sundays, and then fuck the living hell out of her afterwards. Don't let the bum knee fool you, sweetheart, I can still rock your world, one-legged." He winks. "Honestly, it sounds like a great three-month rest and recovery plan to me. Bulletproof."

I can't speak. It's too good to be true.

"Maybe you'll even get to play Elphaba one night when I'm there, and I'll be able to see it," Tyler adds.

Okay, I can't let that comment go without setting him straight. "I won't get to play Elphaba, babe. I'm third understudy. The Apocalypse would have to happen for me to get the call."

"You never know. One night, Elphaba might get laryngitis and the first two understudies might both inexplicably come down with a mysterious case of diarrhea on that very night." He puts his pinky to his mouth and cocks his eyebrow like Dr. Evil.

I giggle. "Are you sure about this?"

"Absolutely, positively, one hundred percent sure. The stars are perfectly aligned, baby. Let's turn lemons into lemonade."

I squeal with glee. "And after the tour, we'll come back here, and I'll start at the University of Miami. *Perfect.*"

He suddenly looks annoyed.

Oh. My stomach clenches. *Crap.* I guess I should have asked Tyler if he's willing to foot the bill for my tuition and expenses before assuming it. "I shouldn't have assumed you'd pay for my schooling," I say quickly. "I'm sorry. I can totally apply for financial aid."

Tyler rolls his eyes. "Don't be ridiculous, Zooey. I'll pay for anything and everything you want to do in life, whatever it is. You're mine, baby. I'm gonna take care of you from now on, no matter what."

I blush. "Thank you."

Tyler grabs my hand. "One day, you'll be my wife and the

mother of my babies, and my money will be yours. That's a given. Never even wonder about that."

Electricity shoots through me. "We're going to have babies?"

"Of course, we are. We've got to have babies. I want to coach my son in pee wee football one day."

"What if we have a girl?"

"Then I'll coach my daughter in pee wee football."

My smile widens. "She may want to take dancing and singing lessons like her mommy. Or, heck, maybe our son will."

Tyler's face lights up. "That'd be amazing either way." He strokes my arm for a moment. "So here's the thing, my eager little beaver. Given the uncertainty of the situation with me right now, it makes no sense for you to apply to a four-year program in Miami. Who knows where I'll be a year from now? It's fifty-fifty the Dolphins will cut me, and I'll have to shop myself as a free agent. And even if I don't get cut, I'll only have a year left on my contract with the Dolphins by then. Hardly a reason for us to make this town our permanent address. I mean, if there were an incredible theater scene here for you, that'd be one thing. But there isn't."

"But there's no alternative. I only came up with the idea so I could be with you and also keep learning and growing and performing at the same time."

"Yeah, I get it. But if you want to be a college girl again, then I say swing for the fences. Go to NYU. Fuck Miami. Shoot for the stars."

The very mention of NYU makes my skin buzz with electricity. "That makes no sense," I say. "Assuming the second time's the charm for me to get in, which isn't a given *at all*, me going to NYU would mean I'd be living in New York while you were living here. Not an option."

"Oh, you'll get in. Now that you've been on a high-profile tour and made Dean's list at UCLA, you're a proven commodity. Plus, I wonder what would happen if I were to give a healthy donation to the NYU theater department and let it be known I felt inspired to give it after seeing an amazing curly-haired girl on the *Wicked* tour who mentioned it was her lifelong dream to attend NYU?" He flashes me a mischievous look.

I giggle. "*Tyler.*"

"If they reject you after all that, then fuck 'em. They don't get to write your story, *you* do. Either way, I'll get us an amazing penthouse apartment in Manhattan with three-sixty views, and we'll split our time between here and there until I can get my ass to New York full-time. There are two teams in New York and a whole bunch a short distance away. I'll figure it out. Plus, we've got off-seasons, don't forget. So we'll make New York our home base and figure everything else out around that. One way or another, one day, we'll both live full-time in New York, I promise. Until then, we'll just make it work. This thing with you and me is a marathon, not a sprint, baby. Now that we both know for sure we're in it for the long haul, we'll do whatever has to be done."

I bite the inside of my cheek. "The thought of us being apart for even short periods makes me feel physically sick."

"Me, too. But you know what makes me feel even sicker? The thought of me being the reason you don't maximize your time on this planet. If you give New York an honest try and things don't pan out for whatever reason, then that's that. We'll have some babies, and you can teach theater at a high school or do community theater or whatever the fuck someone does with a useless theater degree."

We both laugh.

"But I don't think you're going to be happy ten years from now, twenty years from now, if you're thinking, What if?"

I grab his hand and squeeze it. "Thank you."

"Now text your stage manager and tell her you'll be there tomorrow night. I need probably another week before I can get on an airplane, but you go on ahead. My sister or dad will come hang out with me for a week."

I put my palm on his cheek. "You're an amazing man."

"Bah. It's the halo effect. I'm actually a total dick."

I laugh.

Tyler kisses the top of my hand. "It's all going to work out for us, pretty baby. And you know why? Because we're written in the stars."

I kiss him over and over again. But after a moment, I pull away from him, mute the football game on TV, and grab my phone. "We need a soundtrack for this make-out session. We're going to remember this moment for the rest of our lives, and we need the perfect song for the memory." I quickly navigate to one of my all-time favorite songs—a cheesy song my father told me was one of my mother's favorites: "Never Gonna Give You Up" by Rick Astley.

"Oh, I *love* this song," Tyler says. "It was one of my mom's all-time favorites. Second only to 'Careless Whisper.' She had a thing for cheesy eighties music."

My heart stops. "This was my mom's favorite, too. My dad told me she used to sing it to me all the time."

Emotion washes over Tyler's face. "Well, if that's not a sign we're meant to be, I don't know what is." He kisses me while Rick Astley serenades us, but around midway through the song, Tyler breaks free from my lips. "It's all going to work out," he says, smiling against my lips. "I promise."

"You're incredible."

"It's that damned halo effect."

"Nope. I see you with complete, unfiltered clarity, Tyler, and you're most definitely *not* a dick."

"No, no. I was talking about *your* halo effect, cupcake. It makes me do crazy things to try to impress you. Always has."

I smile broadly. "I love you so much."

"I love you, too."

"I'm so flippin' excited."

"You should be. We're going to have the best life *ever*."

EPILOGUE

"Happy Birthday to youuuuu!"

I clap uproariously. There are two handsome, singing figures at the foot of my bed. The larger one is wearing a T-shirt that reads I Love My Hot Wife. The much smaller figure is wearing a shirt stamped with My Mommy Rocks! "Thank you so much!" I squeal. "Look at all those pancakes! Wow."

"I helped Daddy make 'em," my four-year-old son declares proudly.

Tyler and I exchange a look. He's so dang cute. "Thank you so much, Toby," I say. "Come here."

Toby crawls onto the bed next to me while Tyler sits on the edge of the bed with the tray in his lap.

"I made you a present, Mommy," Toby chirps. He hands me a drawing made in crayon, and immediately, despite the artist's rather loose interpretation of the human form, I know it's meant to be a portrait of our little family. I know this for several reasons. First off, one of the little amoeba-scarecrow-blobs in the drawing has a green face. So, clearly, that's me. I've only recently started playing Elphaba on Broadway after several years of playing in choruses and supporting roles in a myriad of different shows, but Tyler's already proudly taken our son to see his green-faced mommy defy gravity at four matinee performances in a row. But, regardless, even without a green-skinned figure in the drawing, I'd still know it's a portrait of our family because one of the other amoeba-blobs appears to be holding a brown piece of poop in its hands. Which means that's Tyler. And that poop is a football.

The adorable thing is that Toby couldn't possibly remember seeing his father play professional football. Tyler's nine-year NFL career—the last five of which he played with the New York Jets—ended two years ago, when Toby was two. But, still, it's no wonder to me Toby drew his daddy holding a football. Tyler's many football awards and photos and memorabilia grace our sprawling penthouse apartment, right along with my UCLA and NYU memorabilia and framed playbills.

And the final figure in my son's drawing? Well, it's Toby, of course. I know this for certain because his representative blob is smaller than his mommy's and daddy's. Plus, it's holding a football, just like the daddy blob. Not a surprise. There's never been a child on this planet who wants to be more like his daddy than Toby Caldwell.

To be honest, I was kind of hoping my son would show early signs of being a blossoming musical theater geek like me, but it's already quite clear that's a total nonstarter. Toby Caldwell inherited his mother's curly hair and nothing else. In every way, other than that boy's hair, he's his daddy's mini-me, through and through.

"I love it, bubba," I say, looking up from my son's birthday gift to me. "Thank you so much. I'll put it on the fridge."

Tyler props up my pillows behind me and moves to place

the breakfast tray over my lap.

"Hang on," I say. "I've got to run to the bathroom first." I hop out of bed and pad across the room. "Make sure Daddy saves me a pancake, bubba. You know how much Daddy loves eating all the pancakes."

Toby giggles. It's our family's joke. Daddy and Toby always eat all the pancakes except one. Honestly, I don't even like pancakes, so one saved pancake won't rock my world, especially given the yummy looking yogurt parfait I spied on the tray next to the pancakes. But Toby doesn't need to know my honest feelings about pancakes. All he needs to know at his age is that he always dutifully saves a pancake for his mommy because he's a thoughtful and kind little boy who loves his mommy.

I close the bathroom door behind me, my heart pounding, and grab a pregnancy test from under my sink. It's been torture waiting for today to take this test. But I wanted to wait long enough to confidently avoid a false negative. And then I had the brilliant idea to wait an extra week until my birthday morning to find out.

I pee on the stick and put it on the ledge of the sink, assuming I'm going to have to wait a few minutes for the result. But, almost instantly, a bright pink "plus" sign begins appearing in the result pane. I clap my hand over my mouth. *Oh, my God.* Tyler's going to freak. He's been wanting another Caldwell for three years. I hide the stick behind my back and saunter into the bedroom.

"What the heck?" I shriek, feigning shock at the lone pancake sitting on the tray. "What happened to all the pancakes?"

Toby squeals with laughter. He looks at his daddy, and they share a guilty smile. "I told Daddy not to eat that one because it's your birthday, Mommy."

"Thank you. Glad to know *someone* around here has some self-restraint." I sit on the bed and pick up my son's drawing again. "Hey, bubba, do you think you'd be willing to add something to your drawing for me? I think there's a little something missing."

Toby looks perplexed. But Tyler's face instantly lights up like a Christmas tree.

"What?" Toby asks, scooting next to me on the bed to look at the drawing. His little brow is knitted.

I gaze at Tyler to find him looking like he's holding his breath. "A baby brother or sister," I say, pulling the pee stick out from behind my back with a giggle.

"Oh, babe," Tyler says. He grabs my face and kisses me with so much fervor, he takes my breath away. "The Caldwells are multiplying!" he shouts, raising his fist in victory. "You're gonna be a big brother, Toby! Mommy's got a little brother or sister inside her belly right now."

"In there?" He pokes me.

"In there," I confirm.

Toby nods like all's right with the world. "Good," he says matter-of-factly. "I'll play football with Daddy, and our baby will sing and dance with Mommy and everyone will have a best friend."

Tyler and I laugh.

"How sweet of you to want a best friend for me," I say. I

wipe a pancake crumb off my son's lip with my thumb. "Thank you, bubba."

My eyes drift to Tyler, and my clit pulses at the sight of him. Holy hot damn. My husband looks sexy as hell right now. Clearly, my baby news has turned him on.

Tyler rustles Toby's curly hair. "Hey, bubba. Let's go find Lucinda, okay? Daddy wants to give Mommy a special birthday present for a little bit. And then we'll all go out together and go ice skating at the rink for Mommy's birthday before she has to go to the theater."

"Okay."

Tyler turns his back toward the edge of the bed, and Toby leaps onto his daddy's back without needing to be told what to do.

"I'll be right back, Mrs. Caldwell," Tyler says over his shoulder. And off he goes with his son on his back to find our live-in housekeeper somewhere in our sprawling apartment. Two minutes later, my husband returns with a wicked gleam in his eyes.

Tyler quietly closes and locks our bedroom door behind him, picks up the tray of food off my lap, and places it on a nearby table. He then proceeds to pull off every stitch of his clothes, gracing me with the view of him that will never get old as long as I live.

"Happy birthday, baby," Tyler says, pulling my pajama bottoms down. He leans down and presses his lips softly against my belly button. "Hello, Baby Caldwell. I can't wait to meet you."

I lean back into my pillows, smiling as my naked husband

crawls onto the bed next to me, pulls my underwear off, and begins trailing kisses from my belly downward. "Happy birthday to me," I whisper softly as Tyler's lips begin doing wondrous things to me. "Happy, *happy* birthday to me."

ALSO AVAILABLE FROM
WATERHOUSE PRESS

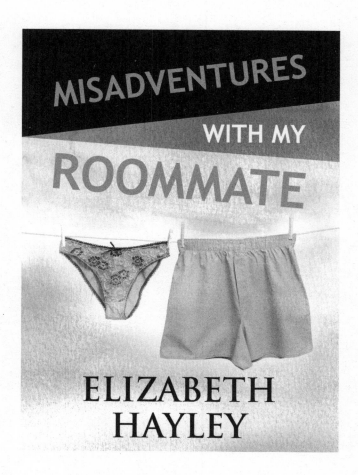

MISADVENTURES
WITH MY
ROOMMATE

ELIZABETH
HAYLEY

Keep reading for an excerpt!

EXCERPT FROM
MISADVENTURES WITH MY ROOMMATE

Gavin threw open the door to The Coffee Bean with more force than was necessary. He scanned the store, thankful it was mostly empty of customers. Then he looked behind the counter, and he was even more thankful. Blake was standing there tying the strings of her black apron around her small waist. It actually would've been difficult to tell just how thin she was if it weren't for the small pieces of fabric that cinched her shirt just under her chest.

Yesterday, Gavin had to force himself not to be a total perv and stare at her all day. Her terrific body, her wavy dark auburn hair that fell over her shoulders, her light-blue eyes, that smattering of freckles on her nose... She was beautiful. The fact that she seemed to have almost no filter was also attractive. Gavin had learned the hard way over the past few years that people rarely said what they meant or were honest about their intentions. In Gavin's world, Blake was a welcome anomaly.

"Hey, hotness," she shamelessly called out when she saw him.

He felt heat prick his face and couldn't help the shy

smile that quirked his lips. Giving her a small wave, he dipped into the back to clock in and grab an apron. When he came back out front, tying his apron as he walked, he approached Blake. "Ready?" he asked.

"For...?"

He barked out a laugh, and damn did it feel good. He didn't laugh nearly enough anymore. "To learn how to make these drinks."

A look of disappointment crossed her features. "Oh. That's not nearly as fun as what I was thinking."

"I bet it wasn't." He shook his head at her brazenness even though he liked it.

He showed her where the recipe book was that she could reference if she got stuck. Then he explained the most common orders and a few variations of each.

"How does anyone remember all this?" she asked, her eyes wide.

Gavin shrugged. "Repetition. Most of these get ordered multiple times a day, so it becomes second nature. And the rare ones you can look up."

"I don't think my brain has room for all of this. I've been a bartender for four years, and I still don't remember how to make most of the drinks. I just throw whatever in a glass, and people know better than to complain."

He smiled again. "What happens if they complain?"

"I throw them out."

Eyebrows shooting up, Gavin said, "*You* throw people out?"

She widened her stance and put a hand on her hip.

"What does that mean?"

"Can we pretend I never said that?"

Blake seemed to mull that over before dropping her arm. "Sure."

Gavin was dumbstruck for a second. "Wait. Really?"

Blake leaned a hip against the counter. "Yeah. I say shit I shouldn't all the time, so it'd be hypocritical of me to hold someone else accountable for the stupid things they blurt out."

Gavin thought there was an insult in there somewhere, but he didn't dwell on it. "Oh. Great. Thanks."

Blake nodded. "So let's talk about more interesting things."

"Like what?"

"Like you."

Trying to keep his face blank so she wouldn't pick up on just how much he *didn't* want to talk about himself, he asked, "What do you want to know?"

She tapped a finger against her chin for a few beats before answering. "Boxers or briefs?"

He rolled his eyes with a chuckle. When he saw her eyes alight with mischief, he decided she was teasing and didn't answer.

"Okay, a real question," she said. "How old are you?"

"Twenty-five," he answered.

"I'm twenty-six. I can be your sugar mama," she joked.

At least he thought she was joking. "Wouldn't be a hard position to qualify for," he said in an attempt to tease her back.

But her face grew serious, making it plain that he'd somehow missed the mark. She looked pensive as she studied him. "What qualifications would someone need? In case I find someone interested in applying."

Gavin laughed again, but it was humorless this time. "Right now, I'd settle for having a couch I could crash on." He wasn't sure why he was being so honest. He didn't need anyone knowing about his personal shit. But part of him wanted to get it off his chest, throw it out into the universe so he didn't have to carry it all on his own. Which was stupid, but he couldn't take it back now.

Blake's eyes grew wide as she bounced on her toes a little. "Oh my God, do you need a place to live? Say yes. Please, please, please say you're homeless."

Gavin had never seen someone so excited by the prospect of his homelessness. Even his parents hadn't seemed to take any actual joy in it, and they'd caused it in the first place.

He busied himself with restocking the cups as he answered. "Not yet. But in about a week I will be if I don't find something. But don't worry. I always land on my feet."

Blake grinned widely. "Well, it actually seems like you've landed right in my lap."

Gavin wasn't sure what that meant, but it sounded both dirty and promising.

◆ ◆ ◆ ◆

Blake couldn't believe her luck. Bethany's dad had shown up at the crack of dawn that morning to help her move her out. Luckily, most of the furniture was Blake's, since she was the constant in the apartment. Her roommates were the revolving door.

Bethany threw her things into garbage bags, and she and her dad carted them out and down the three flights of stairs without saying much of anything to Blake. Blake had nearly had to tackle Bethany to get the key to the apartment back. A key she'd shoved into her pocket and fingered now as she gazed excitedly at Gavin.

"Do I want to know what that means?" Gavin asked.

"I sure hope so." She clapped her hands. "This is so amazing. I'm really going to get to be a sugar mama. Though not really, because you'll need to pay rent. It's pretty cheap though. Four hundred a month. You're not going to find a better deal. So what do you say?"

Gavin's eyes narrowed. "Say to what?"

"Moving in with me! My roommate moved out this morning, so you could move in immediately. She already paid for September, so you wouldn't even need to pay until October."

"You want me to move in with you?" he asked. He sounded confused, which she couldn't understand. She thought she was being pretty damn clear.

"Yes. It'll be perfect. I was just telling my friend Celeste how I should find a male roommate because the girls never last. And now here you are. It's like fate."

"Why do the girls not last?"

Uh-oh. This was exactly the kind of situation where Blake needed to slow down and think before she spoke. But she didn't. "Because I can be a little...much."

Gavin's eyes flashed with unease.

"But not like, serial-killer much," Blake added in a hurry. "I'm not hiding bodies in the floorboards or anything. But I am a tad eccentric. It becomes endearing after a while. You can ask my friend Celeste." Celeste had recommended Blake refer to herself as eccentric instead of saying she was "batshit crazy," which was off-putting. *Go figure.*

She eyed Gavin anxiously as he seemed to think over his options.

"So I could move in immediately?"

Trying to tamp down the flare of hope, she kept her voice even. "Yup."

Gavin thought for another moment before extending his hand in her direction. "Then you got yourself a roommate."

"Yay," she said as she ignored his hand and jumped into his arms for a hug.

"I have a feeling my life is about to get very interesting," he mumbled against her cheek.

She squeezed him tighter. "Probably. But in all the best ways."

***This story continues in
Misadventures with My Roommate!***

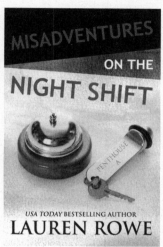

MORE MISADVENTURES

A NOTE FROM LAUREN

Anyone who knows me is well aware I'm a diehard football fan. I also happen to be a UCLA Bruin who bleeds blue and gold. And that means I was brainwashed in my highly formative years to despise our cross-town rivals, the Trojans of USC. So, to anyone from that sparkling, private institution across town who might have been rankled to see my darling Zooey talking some serious trash about you guys at a fictitious football game, not to mention having to read about my Bruins soundly beating your sorry cardinal and gold booties at said fictitious game, I want to extend a (completely disingenuous) apology to you for any offense caused. It was all in good fun, my dear, rivalrous friend. Thank you so much for reading my story! (And Go Bruins!)

MUSIC PLAYLIST

"Come & Go" — *Pitbull*

"Let's Get It On" — *Marvin Gaye*

"I'll Make Love to You" — *Boyz II Men*

"I Want Your Sex" — *George Michael*

"Pour Some Sugar on Me" — *Def Leppard*

"Crash into Me" — *Dave Matthews Band*

"Enter Sandman" — *Metallica*

"Flagpole Sitta" — *Harvey Danger*

"Careless Whisper" — *George Michael*

"Defying Gravity" — *Idina Menzel, from Wicked*

"Alive" — *P.O.D.*

"Hallelujah" — *Leonard Cohen, as covered by Jeff Buckley*

"Never Gonna Give You Up" — *Rick Astley*